an unfinished coloring book   Cameron Cowan

II

Copyright © Widgery Omnimedia and Cameron Cowan 2020
Seattle, Washington

cameronjournal.com
Printed in America

ISBN: 978-0-578-64958-0

Acknowledgements

Nana
Mom and Dad
Liz Williams (who edited the collection)

Trigger Warnings

Sexual abuse
Drug abuse

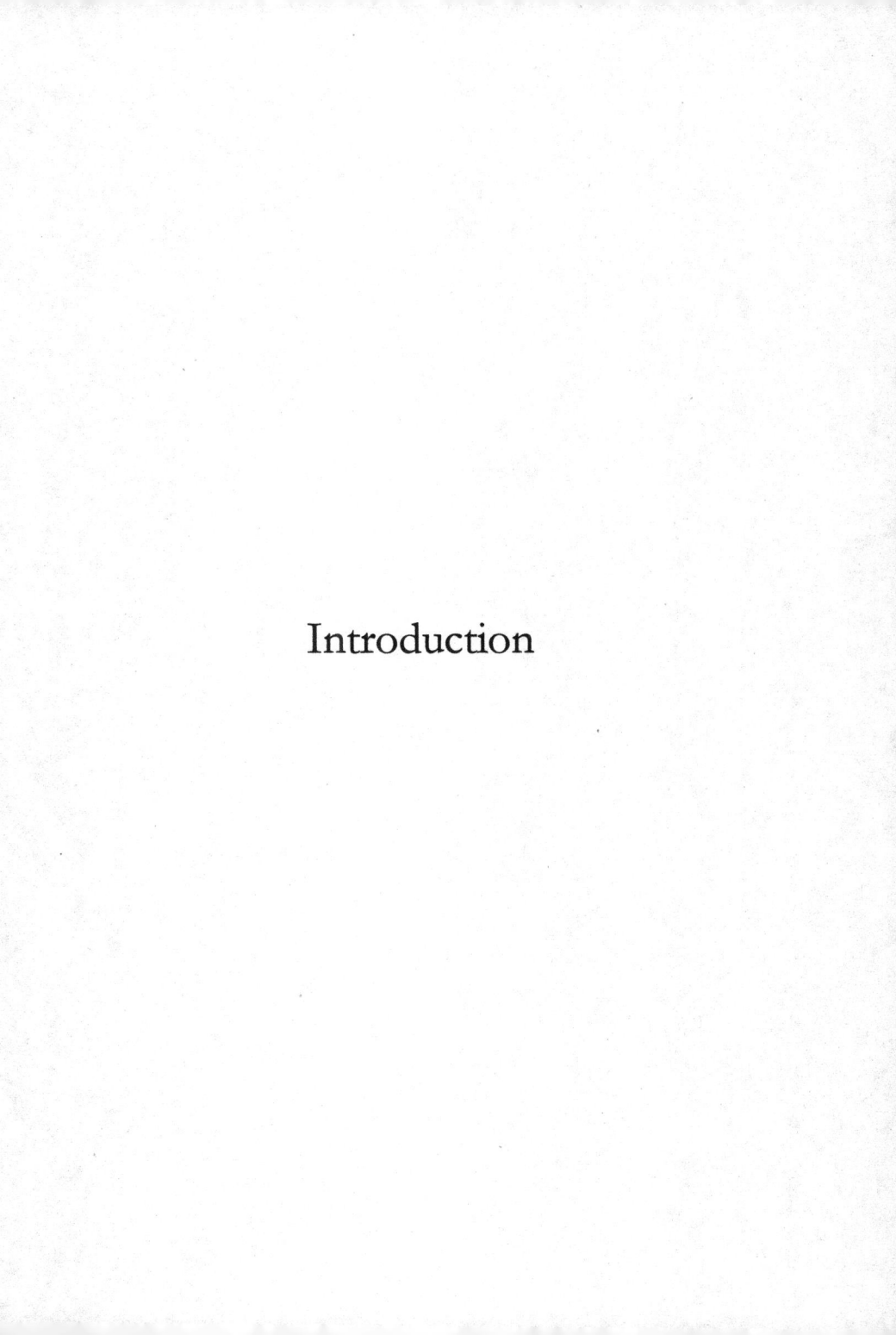

Introduction

This short story collection is exciting for me because when I started writing, I started writing short stories. I would make up characters based on things I'd heard on old time radio and see how I could set them off on adventures. The short story form is an interesting one. I try to use it as a way to provide a momentary snapshot into a single moment or thought process. I always thought that short stories would do very well in our modern age of short attention spans. However, I've not seen them take off the way I thought they would. On the bright side, it means that that people are still digging into deep stories.

This collection is about people and their lived experiences, my favorite story to tell. We all find ourselves in different places in life. Everyone has a story and most of them are worth telling. Sadly, most of the time we will never hear them. Life is a constant state of overcoming. Sometimes it's financial difficulties or a toxic relationship. For others it has to do with ongoing or sudden health problems. Others have to overcome family situations that did not help launch them into life. Sometimes we have to fight the system or fight society as such.

Life is often a battle for survival and some people seem to have a simple time of surviving while others struggle to fulfill even the most basic needs. Life is mysterious and it lacks certainty. We often have to live into the answer of our worries and problems. Some problems are stubborn and just won't go away, while others often resolve themselves and days later we wonder why we ever worried about them in the first place. Modern life is a complicated place. We live in a world where nothing seems certain and everything is changing seemingly all at once. Our modern world is a place where we have to tackle income inequality, the housing crisis, humanitarian problems both within our countries and around the world. The stable order of the world is being upended on a daily basis. It's hard to know what is going on. Even in our daily lives we are facing new challenges that were different for previous generations or even previous parts of our lives. Throughout the collection, I've compiled stories that have to do with loss and with overcoming because that is what people face. Many people have to face up to challenges within themselves and within society and find their own way. Sometimes we face our own demons and other times we have to face outside forces that threaten our own survival.

Not everyone makes it. In many stories, the conclusion is that the detective always finds the murderer and justice is served. However, real life isn't always so easy. Sometimes a miscarriage of justice leaves someone in jail wrongfully. Sometimes the murderer is never caught. People lose their homes. At other times, we are powerless before forces greater than ourselves and the best we can do is simply accept what has happened.

This collection is called "the unfinished coloring book" because I firmly believe that life is like an unfinished coloring book. Each choice is a color and we fill in certain sections of certain pages and we can end up with a book full of half finished pages. Each page represents a road that we went down that didn't work out. However, on occasion, we make all the right color choices and we end up with that completed page. That's when the stars align and everything goes just right. The moment of finishing that page is a sweet moment because we get that wonderful accomplishment of seeing the whole page as we envisioned it in our head. On occasion life offers us those moments. However, it takes many unfinished pages to get there and we are still being colored in until the moment our consciousness shifts to whatever comes next and the color book is closed in whatever state of completion it is in at that time.

In this collection I drew together a variety of stories to take us towards different moments and to look at life, those unfinished pages, from a variety of angles. In this collection we travel from broken relationships to apocalyptic futures and back to the center of the modern crisis.

Enjoy your exploration of the unfinished coloring book.

Table of Contents

The Diner

Vince spread some Shea butter lotion on his dark skin and replaced the lotion in his backpack. He looked down at his phone and tapped the screen, texting his wife in between bites of food right before his late-night shift started. The Diner was empty right now but he knew the regulars would be streaming in soon. He put on his crisp, white apron with its tough but soft-feel fabric and the small cloth hat with black lines. The ring of the doorbell abruptly interrupted his musing and text messaging. He walked out of the short, plastic-walled hallway that connected the main dining area and kitchen to the small staff and storage area in the back.

Two men - a couple of his nightly regulars - were already sitting down at the long Formica counter, placing their hats on its austere surface. Vince put out silverware on thin bi-fold napkins. The day shift had not prepared the tables at all. It was the last night and the day shift didn't care anymore. The floor and tables were covered in a kind of Formica laminate from the 70's, the last time the Diner had been remodeled. The yellow and brown counter matched the yellow and brown tables. The yellow part indicated where the plates and eating should take place and a small square for condiments and a circle for the glass. The edges were covered in metal and the old red original barstools had been replaced with brown ones with short backs.

Old pictures of the Diner showed the old wood paneling that had disappeared in the 90's. The walls now were drywall with pictures and posters of various bands, events and things gone by. Vince put out two thin menus although he already knew what they were going to order.

"What'll it be, gentlemen?"

"The usual. We don't change much."

"Sounds great, coming right up. Cookie! Two eggs medium and sausage, two eggs scrambled well, chicken fried steak, sourdough toast, two pancakes and hash browns all around."

"Yeah, yeah, I'm on it! Is Jose coming in tonight?"

"Sounds like the usual mood!" one of the men remarked.

"Of course." Vince turned around towards the open pass through to the kitchen, "And no, Cookie - no Jose tonight - he called in," Vince said with a laugh.

"Is it true?" one of the men asked.

"What?" Vince asked.

"That this is it - this is the last night?"

"Yeah, it's true and that's why there's no Jose to wash dishes," Vince said simply.

"What are you going to do?"

"About the dishes? Wash them myself, I guess."

"No, about a j-o-b."

"I don't know." Vince walked over to the condiments bar and brought over bottles of ketchup, sriracha, mustard and Tabasco.

"Don't you have another little one on the way?"

"Yeah, Chante is really happy about it."

"But how are you going to support them?"

"I'll have to find a new job. Maybe they'll build something alongside the new interstate."

"Maybe."

The men took out their newspapers and started leafing through them.

"Food's up!" Cookie called as he rang the bell.

Vince buttered the toast and as he set the plates down, swapped out the jelly container. He grabbed the fullest syrup container. He pulled out the tray to fill the rest of them for later. The men put down their newspapers and started to eat, chatting in between bites.

"I just can't believe that they're tearing this place down. It's an institution."

"Yeah, it really does mean a lot to people," Vince said as he looked around the room.

"Doesn't it mean a lot to you? You've worked here for several years - you were the busboy when you were in high school."

"It does mean a lot to me, but I will admit, Chante and I are thinking about moving."

"Ah, yeah, a lot of kids move away these days."

"Been happening for years," the old man's partner finally piped in.

"You eat too fast, Ed - you should enjoy the food. Ain't gonna be getting it again."

"Oh hush up Robert, you always eat slow. If I ate as slow as you do that's all we'd do, eat."

"Take your time gentlemen, I'll get the check," Vince smiled. He wrote out the ticket and totted up the amount for the men. He thought about Chante's growing belly at home and how hard it was going to be to get another job. Vince put the ticket on the counter between the two of them.

"Ed, pay the bill."

"Robert, I paid the last time, it's your turn."

"OK, give me your card."

"That's still me paying!" Robert sighed and pulled out a wad of cash from his pocket and pulled out two twenty dollar bills. He held them up and put them on the check.

"Vince, this is for you."

"Thank you, Mr. Robert."

The men finished their coffee in near silence. Robert put down his coffee first, got up, put on his hat and adjusted his medium wash Levi's. Ed got up next and put his hat on. The two men joined hands, got two toothpicks and left the Diner hand in hand.

The Diner was quiet again. Food sizzled on the grill as Cookie made himself some food. Vince refilled all the condiments and syrups and put them out on the tables. It would save him time during the bar rush. He wiped down the long counter and it reflected the light, making the Diner just a little brighter. Vince had just put the wash rag back into the bleach bucket when a man, no more than forty, in a flashy suit, walked in and sat down at the bar. His phone was out and he was texting furiously.

"Good evening, sir!" Vince put out his silverware and a menu. The man put up a hand in acknowledgement but kept texting away. Vince went back to cleaning.

"Girls are crazy, man!" the man said, finally looking up from his phone.

"They can be, sir. How can I help you tonight?"

"Coffee would be great!" he said as he turned over the menu looking for something to eat.

"I'm surprised that you're here," Vince said pouring out the coffee into the cup.

"Why?"

"You arranged for this place to be torn down," Vince said replacing the carafe of coffee into the machine.

"I just brokered the deal and delt with the paperwork. That's my job man."

Vince shook his head, "Lawyers," Vince said with a sigh.

"I've heard all the jokes."

"Do you know what you'd like to eat?"

Cookie was out back, smoking. He leaned against the brick. His shoe rested on the rusty flashing near the ground. He inhaled the light smoke and exhaled with regularity. He didn't have another job lined up - there weren't many jobs for felons. Food was a hard industry, but for him, it was the only industry with enough turnover to forgive rape of a minor, assault, and battery with a deadly weapon. He flicked the cigarette butt into the six spot parking lot, then opened the metal safety door and went down the short hallway past the required employment posters to the hand-washing sink. He scrubbed his hands. Would he try to rape a girl tonight? What would he have to lose? His life was coming to an end like the walls of the Diner. Prison seemed like a welcome respite. He wondered if his girlfriend ever thought about the fact that the same penis that raped that twelve year old girl while her mother looked on in horror was the same member she wrapped her lips around every night? This job was the only reason he hadn't "reoffended," as his probation officer put it. But without the job, why shouldn't he? What was his incentive? What was society doing for him? He could imagine it now, his manhood stiffened. The shock and horror, the feeling of power and control, it wasn't the sex that mattered. The act was about his ability to do it and he licked his lips at the thought. He could rob that little girl of something that she didn't know she valued until it was gone.

"Two eggs over hard, two bacon!" Vince shouted. His train of thought was broken as he made his way into the kitchen, put the grill on higher and started the order. It was time to focus.

"It's really a shame that an old place like this had to be in the way of the new interstate," the lawyer said as he smiled.

Vince smiled weakly. "It didn't have to be - you helped decide that."

"Hey now, don't worry, there will be tons of new jobs around the exits. You'll find something."

"Yeah, so I can do this job for minimum wage at a corporate place?"

"Maybe you should get out of food?"

"What else am I supposed to do?"

"Oh, I don't know man, go back to school, find something you like," the friendly lawyer encouraged.

"Order up!" Cookie announced with a bell ring.

"I got kids, man, I don't know if school is going to fit in anytime. Here's your order, two eggs over well, toast, two orders of bacon and orange juice. Anything else, sir?"

"No, thank you."

"Let me know if you need anything else." The lawyer loosed his tie and started eating. A few minutes later he cursed. He spilled egg on his tie.

"$400, fucking A!" Vince brought him a glass of ice water.

"You might be able to dab it out." The lawyer took it off.

"I'll just buy another one." He kept eating. After his last bite he put a $50 bill on the counter and got up to leave. Vince asked him for change.

"Keep it," he said.

He put up a peace sign as he walked out the metal frame glass door and walked out into the night. Vince looked at him sit down in his BMW coupe, shift in the gear and peel out of the driveway. Vince cleaned up and put the dishes in the washer and sanitizer. Silence fell over the Diner and Vince leaned against the counter, looking for his next customer. A woman, heavily pregnant, came into the Diner and sat down at a chair at the table by the door. Vince hurried out with a menu and a glass of water.

"How are you doing tonight, ma'am?"

"I am doing well, and yourself?"

"Good, thank you. Our special this evening is the flatiron

steak with potatoes or eggs and vegetables or hash browns depending on your desire for breakfast or dinner."

"Thank you, I'll just have chicken fried steak with potatoes and veggies with some Iced Tea."

"Right away." Vince walked back behind the counter. "Chicken fry, spuds, and greens!" Vince poured the glass of iced tea and brought it to the table.

"Do you have Equal?"

"Sure, I guess those didn't get refilled." Vince found some Equal packets and filled the little dispenser. The lady took out three and poured them into her tea. She took a few sips and seemed pleased. Vince stood behind the counter waiting for the order to be up. The lady began to hold her stomach. Sweat formed on her brow and she was fanning herself. Vince, concerned, walked around to check in on her. "Is everything alright?"

"Oh, yessir, thank you for asking. I'm due any day so it's just some cramping. My little one is just goin' crazy in there!"

"Ah ha, well, let me know if there is anything I can do." Vince returned to his place behind the counter. The lady got up and went to the bathroom. A few minutes later she came back out with a worried look on her face. She got out her phone and started to make a few calls. She dialed several numbers but no one responded. She held her stomach and breathed heavily.

"Order up!"

Vince turned around to her dinner, sitting there under the heat lamp. Vince garnished it with some parsley and ran the food out.

"Ma'am, Chicken Fried Steak, mashed potatoes, gravy and greens."

"Thank you, thank you very much." She ate quietly by herself. She was about halfway through her meal when there was a steady drip, drip, drip under her table. She looked worried as her hand felt her body.

"Oh God," she said as a cramp struck her.

"Excuse me?" Vince hurried over.

"Thank you, I am so sorry, but my water just broke all over your floor, can you help me to the bathroom? I need to call 911, I think it's time!"

"Of course!" Vince held her hand and she gingerly stood up and made her way to the bathroom. She had her phone and started to dial 911 as another contraction rippled through her body. Vince led her to the bathroom and ran around back for some towels. He knocked on the door, towels in hand.

"Yes, come in!"

"Here are some towels, ma'am if you need them. When did they say they were going to be here?"

"Twenty minutes according to the lady at the dispatch."

"That's a long time! The baby could be here by then."

"Let's hope he don't come that soon! Do you have any children?"

"Yes ma'am, a daughter."

"Will you stay with me?"

"Of course, ma'am, let's make you as comfortable as possible. Do you want a chair?"

"Yes, that would be nice." Vince retrieved a chair from the dining room and took it into the bathroom. He covered it in a few towels and helped the woman onto it.

"Have you timed the contractions?"

"I think I've had two contractions about ten minutes apart now."

"Ah, then we have some time. Keep breathing. I'll get some water."

"Could you bring me my iced tea?"

"Of course." Vince gathered a glass of water and the glass of iced tea and freshened it.

"Is she going to have her baby in there?" Cookie asked as Vince rushed back to the bathroom.

"I don't know, I hope not." Vince returned with the water and tea.

"More contractions!" she said, exasperated.

"How long since you called 911?"

"About ten minutes!"

"Where are they?"

"I don't know, but if they don't hurry the baby is going to come right here!"

"I know, I know." The woman removed her shoes and began to remove her pants. Vince started to leave.

"It's OK. You don't have to leave."

"You don't mind?"

"No, no, you've been wonderful!" The woman, naked from the waist down, sat back on the chair. A few tense minutes passed. Vince stood by the door, looking out for the paramedics. The woman was breathing heavily. Her stomach was visibly moving now. Vince held her hand.

"It looks like those contractions are just a few minutes apart," Vince remarked.

"Yes, that's right." She breathed heavily. A few more tense minutes passed.

"It's going to be OK. I was with my wife when she had our daughter, so I know a little bit about this kind of thing."

"That's good! Can you look?"

"Uh, sure." Vince bent down further and looked between her legs. She held them far apart.

"Nothing yet, that's good for them getting here." A knock at the door broke the spell in the bathroom.

"Paramedics!"

"Come in please!" she said in between breaths. The paramedics rushed in. Vince switched to her left side.

"How far apart are the contractions?"

"About two minutes now."

"OK, let's get you onto the gurney." The paramedics helped the woman into the flat gurney. They wheeled the woman out, got her out to the ambulance and closed the doors. The ambulance didn't move for several minutes. The doors opened one last time. One of the paramedics jumped down and walked into the Diner. The woman opened the door but didn't come in.

"She wanted me to tell you, thank you for all your help. She just had a baby boy. She also wanted to see how much for dinner."

Vince smiled, "Tell her it was my pleasure and it's on the house. Can I get you anything?"

"Not right now, we have to take her to the hospital but we may be back for something to eat."

"Right on." Vince smiled at the friendly paramedic and waved as she left.

Vince spent the next few minutes cleaning the bathroom. The white surfaces sparkled in no time. Vince looked around the bathroom with a feeling of satisfaction. By this time next week, all of this would be on a roll-off dumpster. But for now, he had the unique satisfaction of having it clean.

Cookie opened the door. "We got customers, man."

Vince put up the "wet floor" sign and put the cleaning supplies away, quickly washed his hands and started taking the first few orders of the bar rush. The big clock over the counter and in front of the kitchen read 2:15 and people streamed in for food. Vince shouted out orders constantly and Cookie managed the grill with precision as food was plated and ran out almost non-stop for two hours. By 4:00 a.m. the Diner had emptied out with the last patrons, including the paramedics, filtering out. Vince wiped down the bar again. There was a large pile of dishes in the back to wash. He was not looking forward to having to deal with those.

"Thanks, Jose," Vince muttered, looking at the massive pile of dishes. He put the towel down and leaned against the condiments counter. There were two guys loitering outside of the Diner, right near the *no loitering* sign. The shorter man looked professional with a collared shirt and short hair cut. The taller man looked like someone who couldn't dress for his age. He wore a modern looking t-shirt and what looked like shorts with longer hair and a short beard. Both men looked like they were around thirty five but the taller man could have been older.

"Are you going to do something about that?" Cookie asked.

"In a minute. I'm not in the mood." The words had no sooner left his lips than the larger and taller of the two men reached out and punched the other fellow in the face. He was so stunned that he fell to the ground. Vince jumped over the counter and ran out to the sidewalk.

"Get out of here! I'll call the fucking cops!" Vince shouted authoritatively.

The man on the ground got up. The tall man's chest heaved, fists clenched.

"It's OK, I deserved it. I bothered him first." Vince looked at the two men. The tall man held out his arms towards the smaller man and they embraced each other. Vince stood there looking at them.

"Can I offer you gentlemen something to eat?" The three men walked into the Diner. They sat down. Vince put out some menus for them.

"This is a great place," the tall man remarked. "Anything to drink?"

"Vanilla coke," the short man said.

"The same."

"Two Vanilla cokes coming up." Vince filled the coke-bottle

style glasses and added two pumps of vanilla flavoring from the big pump operated bottles and set them in front of the men.

"What can I get for you?"

"I'll have the double hamburger and cheese. Hold the pickles."

"I'll have the chicken club, fries, and ranch for my fries."

"Sounds good, guys. Cookie! Cookie?" Vince went around to the back to see where his cook had gone. He opened the metal door that led to the back parking lot. The cold air from the outside struck his face. Cookie was leaning against the brick wall again. A cigarette burned in his hand as he looked up at the starless sky. Vince let the silence set in.

"What are you thinking about?"

"Kids."

"You shouldn't think like that."

"I'm about to be an unemployed sex offender. Prison looks pretty good right now."

"So they can beat the crap out of you, rape you, and maybe kill you?"

"Better than being homeless."

"Not better - you found this job, you can find a new one."

"I don't know, I just don't know."

"Well I know something."

"What's that?"

"I need a double hamburger add cheese, hold the pickle and a chicken club with fries."

Cookie laughed. "Coming up."

He flicked the cigarette into the parking lot and went to the hand washing sink. The grille fired with food. The men chatted and patted shoulders. Vince looked on and smirked. He brought condiments just as the food arrived.

"Order's up!"

Vince garnished and prepared the plates and set them in front of the customers.

"Double hamburger and bacon, wait no, and cheese, sorry, no pickle and chicken club with fries and ranch."

"Thanks."

"Yeah, thanks."

"Refills?"

"Please."

Vince brought fresh drinks and watched the men eat. The men ate in silence. "I'll let you both eat for free if you can answer one question."

"What's that?" the shorter man asked.

"What was the fight about?"

The tall man laughed. "We used to be friends several years ago."

"Yeah, and then his girlfriend decided to change friends."

"I never really knew who it was but it turns out they got married, had a couple kids and just divorced."

"We ran into each other tonight and got in an argument."

"You know the rest."

Vince folded his arms over his chest and looked at the men. The shorter man had a nice black eye. The pleasant-faced tall man looked happy but was waiting to see if their story had earned them a free meal. Vince shook his head a couple times.

"This is on us, guys." The men gave each other a high-five. Vince went through the small hallway and into the back for some air. Several minutes later, he circled his way around the building and came back in the front door. The men were gone and there was $40 left on the counter with a note on a napkin.

"Thanks for the offer."

Vince pocketed the money, took the dishes, and looked at the clock. It read 5:57. Three minutes until it was all over. Vince went over to the door and locked it and moved the sign to *closed*. He took off his hat and readied himself for all the dishes in the back that needed washing and sanitizing. They would look really good in a Chinese restaurant when the owner sold them. Cookie was already cleaning the kitchen. He could hear him scrape the grill and stack up pans. Vince was in the back, loading the glasses rack into the dishwasher yet again when he heard the front door unlock itself. Vince came out to see who was arriving. A short man of about seventy five with neatly pressed slacks and a plaid shirt re-locked the door behind him.

"Morning, Tom!"

"Morning Vince, how was our last night?"

"It was good, eventful, but good."

Cookie nodded at Tom as he took a stack of small pans to the wash.

"How can I help you? We're already cleaning up, but we might be able to come up with something to eat."

"No, no Vince, I'm not here to eat anything. I'm just here to see you, actually."

"Final paycheck?"

"You could say that." Tom handed Vince an envelope.

"Thank you, very much, it has been a pleasure working here, that's all I can say."

"You're welcome, Vince. Here, can you give this to Cookie?"

"Yeah, no problem, I'll go give it to him right now."

"Thanks Vince, I appreciate it. Hopefully, I'll see you around town."

"I hope so too sir, have a good night!" Tom exited the Diner and Vince re-locked the door. The sun was just peeking over the horizon at 7:15 when he stepped outside from the tedium of washing dishes. He took the envelope out of his back pocket and tore it open.

Pay to the order of: Vincent Williams
Amount: One Hundred Thousand Dollars.

Vince was amazed.

"This has got to be a mistake," he told himself.

Just as Vince was about to call Tom he found a note on the ground that had accompanied the check.

Dear Vince,
No, the check is not a mistake, it is my gift to you for your years of service and will hopefully help you and your wife start a new life.
God Bless, Tom

A single tear rolled down Vince's cheek. Cookie poked his head out the door.

"There you are, how many more loads do you have?"

"Uh, just one or two I think. Should be done pretty quick."

"OK, thanks."

"Uh, here, the boss left your final paycheck for you." Vince handed him the envelope.

"Thanks, I appreciate that." The clock read 8:45 by the time all the dishes had been stacked. The Diner looked ready to serve a breakfast rush that would have been starting any other day. Normally, the morning shift would have already been serving breakfast, chatting with regulars, and wiping tables. But today the sun was shining in on an empty Diner that wouldn't even be there in just a precious few days. Vince pulled out a chair and sat down at a table on the far side. He got a long look at the Diner. It would be his last. Cookie came out into the dining room.

"Did you open your envelope?"

"Yeah, why?"

"The boss gave me five grand!"

"That's good, a nice bonus, it'll help you out."

"Yeah, did he give you anything?"

"Yeah he did, it will help with the new baby."

"That's good, that's real good. Thanks for earlier, I needed that. I'm beat. I'm gonna head home and see my girl before she goes to work."

"Great, man, I'll see you around?"

"Yeah, hopefully."

"Night."

"Night, man." A few minutes later Vince put the chair back up and closed the metal door behind him as he started the walk home to his apartment.

Maybe he would go back to school.

Maybe he would do a lot of things.

The Swedish Connection

Alcohol is a funny thing. When we are young, it is a symbol of adult privilege. It's one of those things that you get to do "when you're older." Much like driving, the first drink is a rite of passage. Many take that rite of passage in secret with their friends in basements, garages, barns, and parks.

Alcohol is a funny thing. It doesn't taste so great at first but young people want to be cool and take advantage of the special privilege so everyone gets used to the taste. For some people it becomes because their reason for living - which is another level of depression caused by some people fermenting and distilling things to create the magic that is alcohol.

I grew up in a house where alcohol wasn't something mysterious. However, caution was due, for alcoholism ran in the family. I remember my first glass of wine. I was seventeen years old and I was standing in the Brown Palace Hotel in Denver. The room looked like an old smoking lounge straight of the 19th century. The walls were covered in wood panelling and the carpet was thick. The staff were dressed in neat black clothing. The scene had a certain air of sophistication and expense. I was working as a legislative aide for a state senator and they didn't ask for my ID. I wore a great suit with my badge and they simply handed me a glass of red wine. It was bitter but I wanted to fit in so I swirled it like the member of clergy I saw in the corner. He looked smart and well-placed in his robes so I thought he was a good example to follow. I swirled the liquid like him and tried not to make a face when the bitter, dry, red wine hit my tongue.

I remember my first legal drink. I was graduating college at just twenty one and it was university funded. The alumni association threw us a party. It was pretty fun, legally drinking on the university dime. A few days before I discovered the joys of legal drinking when a bar had let me in two days early of my birthday and given me a coveted wrist band allowing me to consume. There's something about crossing that barrier that makes you really feel you're an adult. My twenty first birthday party was fun but I didn't do any crazy drinking that night. My first experience with legal drunkenness would come later.

My first proper adult party was interesting. I had forgotten to learn about drinks and what to order so I ordered vintage drinks that I had heard my family talking about. The bartender thought it was pretty strange when a young man who had just turned twenty one was asking for a highball. Fortunately, I was with friends and they taught me how to drink like a modern adult. It was an important part of my education.

Like I said, alcohol is a funny thing. When life goes sideways, we seek out its liquid comfort. The warmth and the cozy feeling that goes along with alcohol gives it a unique appeal. Alcohol is also a deeply social substance. It's best enjoyed with friends. Even lousy alcohol is improved when you're around friends who care about you and who you have a real connection with.

When my phone started blinking and buzzing, I looked under my desk where my phone was tethered to see who was calling. Even though I wasn't planning on answering the phone, I decided to swipe right on the green button to answer this particular friend. He and I were both freelance artists which meant we didn't always have time to hang out. Freelancing is a constant hustle. But we could sit on the phone and work at editing photos and other tasks and that way we could get work done, get paid, and be friends. I figured it was one such call.

"Hello?"

"You have to taste this - this is the cheapest, worst vodka I've ever tasted. You should drive down."

I was sitting at home in my office chair staring at Facebook and Tumblr; friends on one tab, porn on the other. This was back before tumblr forgot what their platform was created to do: share content. I should have been writing but somehow social media has a great deal of appeal when there's work to be done. Judging by my friend's phone call, he was similarly affected. It was one of those nights where life's problems overwhelmed the ability to be creative. We all have our vices and we were indulging in them. Why not do it together?

A few minutes later, I was dragging myself out to my car to make the late night drive all the way into downtown Denver. I pulled my car out into the street and started to navigate through the stoplights down to the highway. I drove over a few roads and onto I-25 before I pulled off at a downtown exit. Traffic was light and soon I was navigating the narrow streets of Capitol Hill to get to his house.

Denver has a certain magic: a modern city with skyscrapers still surrounding its historic past and the houses of the people who had rebuilt the city after the fire of 1853 had burned the entirety of Denver City to the ground. There wasn't a Mrs O'Leary or a cow to blame. They just moved the city to the other side of Cherry Creek. Denver, as it's known today, was built to replace it.

Fortunately, there was rock star parking right in front of the late 19th century house. A nice bit of luck in that neighborhood where garages are rare and everyone parks on the street, especially those going to the bars in the area. I pulled my body, all 285 pounds of light-mocha flesh, out of my little diesel VW New Beetle and onto the pavement. The street was only dotted with a few street lights but my path up the stone steps was lighted by the friendly porch light and a small oil lamp, before which, my friend sat with "the bottle."

"You need to try this…vodka, and I use that term loosely."

My friend was sitting on the aging porch with a bottle of this curious liquid, the aforementioned oil lamp, a small table and a few chairs. Even though it was warm outside, my friend was wearing a leather jacket and some generic jeans. His face sported enough facial hair to tell me it hadn't seen a razor in at least three or four days. The fragrance of his clove cigarettes swam into my nostrils. You always smelt him before you saw him. I sat down on the chair and looked at the bottle in question. I lit a cigarette of my own and added to the tobacco fragrance of the air. I always smoked Nat Sherman Fantasia's. I like the colored papers. I selected blue tonight.

"This isn't vodka," he stated, pointing at the bottle of clear liquid.

I picked up the bottle and looked at the label that read "Curiel." They had clearly hired an expert graphic designer and had spared no expense on the paper or the seamless glue that didn't even show through the slightly frosted glass.

"Says here it's vodka."

"Look this shit up, man, it's not vodka."

I pulled out my iPhone and googled the name. The promotional website was the first link and I tapped on it. The language was vapid. The website talked about the water they used from an unpronounceable Swedish lake and the seemingly complicated process of distilling wheat and grains to create a clear liquid that had been put in this bottle, bought on clearance from the liquor store two blocks away, which was now sitting on the small table for us to talk about it. The words "crisp," "full of body," and "old fashioned flavor" had been used.

"It's grain alcohol. It's basically upscale Everclear."

"I guess it's time to find out."

"Drink up, man."

I dashed into the house for my regular mason jar, which I had tucked away on the top of his fridge. I rinsed it out and came back out to the porch. I poured a little of our questionable liquor in my jar. I swigged it back and my tongue was immediately accosted by the harshness. The liquid burnt my throat all the way down to my stomach. I needed a chaser but nothing was available. Soon enough the burn finally faded with a throaty cough.

"You're right, that is Swedish. Everclear."

"I feel like I need to be somewhere in the Ozarks on a porch drinking this fresh from the still ran by a guy named Bubba."

"Yup."

"I think this is the worst piece of crap vodka I've ever tasted. It was just the cheapest thing there."

"This is bad, man, for sure."

I refilled the oil lamp a few moments later. Even though it was bad, it was what was there so we kept drinking. There is something easy and magical about two men sitting outdoors on a cool May evening, drinking bad vodka, and talking about life. The conversation was easy and natural, if a bit uncomfortable at times. A couple of hours passed and I knew that he needed that Vodka more than I did. I switched to a Pinot Grigio that I stole from his girlfriend, who had left it in their refrigerator.

"I think she's leaving me."

"What's this now?"

"I think she's leaving me, man." He took another shot of the terrible Swedish vodka.

"Why do you think that?"

"I can just tell."

"How?"

"We got in a fight, about stupid shit. I'm pretty sure that she's seeing another guy."

"Did you look through her phone?"

"Not yet. Too afraid." He took another shot from the Everclear.

I lit another cigarette. "That age gap. Will kill it every time."

"I honestly thought it didn't matter," he said, looking up at the exposed beams of the porch and pulling on his shirt. "I could lose some weight," he added, patting his small gut.

"Yeah, I mean I guess. If you think it'll help."

I've always had a theory. Eventually those women move on to someone else. Dating someone in your forties when you are in your twenties sounds like fun for a time. Then it becomes less fun at some point. I think it's because women start doing the math. When they are in their forties, the man they are dating will be in his sixties and so on. Like I said, it's fun until it's not.

"Don't let me forget that I owe her a bottle of my uncle's wine." He nodded at me as I poured the wine into the glass.

"Are you seeing anybody?" he asked me.

"Please, you know I never am. Just the occasional hookup. Dating guys is tough."

"Women love you. I remember all those models hanging off, just treating you like a couch. You should date women more."

I nodded and ashed my cigarette. "Maybe, I get weird sometimes."

As the night went on, we moved back inside. Dark swept over the desert plain and the street lights offered a gentle, if sparse, glow onto the streets below. We kept talking while I made a thorough search of the parlor. I listened to him dole out advice and call me a few names as I laid on the original wood floors of the distressed Victorian interior and searched under the furniture for something he was missing. He was always full of life advice about how to promote my career, date more, and be a better man. He liked to talk about my flaws or just be more straight than I was normally. He was a man of a certain generation. I think he was avoiding his own. I don't know why I let him do it but I did. I always left his place feeling down on myself and I could already tell this was going to be one of those nights. By 4 a.m. the bottle of Swedish Everclear had been long gone. I was sitting on his chez lounge looking up at the ceiling nursing my first real cigarette in several months.

"Are you sober?"

"Not really."

"Do you want to sleep?"

"Give me an hour to get straight."

"You're a bisexual, black man, are you ever straight?"

"Three days a week." He laughed at the cheap joke and I just smiled. By 5 a.m. his girlfriend had finally arrived and I was just going out so that I could get back home before the morning rush hour traffic made the trip longer than necessary. The night had been interesting, it had been enlightening, and it was the kind of night that leaves one reflective as the sun came up and my head hit my pillow.

The Kingdom of Nordstrom

The rain pelted against the blue fabric of the tarp. Beads of moisture ran off onto the ground. Inside the shelter, Jon rolled over one more time, hoping for a few more precious minutes of sleep. He finally rolled onto his back and opened his eyes to the green fabric of the tent.

"Fuck."

He lifted his thin body up onto his elbows. The day was grey; it didn't even look like the sun had come up yet. He used his gloved fingers to dust himself off, slipped on his gas mask and scooted outside the tent to look around. He opened up the first flap of the tent and put on his mask. Then he opened the second flap to the open air. He took his binoculars out of his pack and surveyed the area. He didn't see any movement and, replacing the device, decided to get around to the business of breakfast. He stepped back into the tent, removed his gas mask and moved into the bigger area of the tent.

Breakfast consisted of some oatmeal and dried fruit. He only had to heat a small amount of water in order to get it hot enough for the oatmeal. He was ready to find something indoors and sheltered so that he could quit using his mask and set up a better filtration system than the one he'd attached to the side of his tent. He just had to find the right spot. He pulled out a map he had found in an abandoned convenience store several days before and looked for a path. He saw something promising in the distance. He had never really checked out what was happening at the old Mall. It had taken him quite awhile just to get to the Puget Sound in the first place after the massacre. The Mall seemed like a place where some supplies might be found. That was his destination. Perhaps, something would work as a more permanent shelter.

"The only way to find out is to start riding," he said confidently to himself behind his mask. He undid the twine holding the blue tarp onto the bushes around his small campsite. The tent was next. He carefully and compactly rolled all of this and lashed it to his backpack before mounting his motorcycle. With a kick downward he started the bike and started riding. He rolled over the uneven roads and dodged some abandoned cars. Most cars had been dismantled for their parts or their gas at this point. Valuable things like air filters and tires were gold in the various black markets that had sprung up. The system had taken a huge blow. Jon had no doubt that the world would come crashing back in.

But for now, he was looking for some long-term shelter and foraging chances. The Mall seemed like a good place to do that. He turned past an empty intersection when he stopped short. A large doe was grazing peacefully in the distance. Jon slung his pack off and seized his weapon from the front of his motorcycle and chambered a round as he aimed down the weapon. He counted and exhaled a breath with the bullet. The doe slumped over, unaware of what had just happened to her. Jon rode towards the doe and pulled up near her. He climbed a small knoll before beginning the dressing, separating the meat from the skin and reducing the meat parts to their smallest size. Tonight he would build a smoker and smoke the meat with some salt. Packing up the meat, he returned to his bike and kept going. So far, this plan of action was working out well.

By midday he had finally reached his target. The signs and other familiar markers had fallen or gone. The building was intact. That was a good sign. He parked his bike and looked at the white exterior. The cars looked like they had been near a bad neighborhood. Like the others on the road, anything valuable had long been removed. Jon looked for an entrance and found a wide one where the doors had been broken or removed, then piloted his bike into the Mall. The interior was dark and he lit his headlamp to see, along with the light from the bike. He rode slowly across the tile floor. Displays and kiosks had been pushed aside. Products were strewn about.

Jon rode down the wide corridors. He looked around for likely places to set up, where he might be able to create some space for himself with some good air. Inside, he decided to take off his gas mask and see how the air tasted. He pulled off the rubber mask: the air was fresh and clean, he would have to test it, but that was promising. He kept riding forward, looking for the perfect spot to sleep, rest, recover but which also had access to the outside to smoke his meat. He looked around and realized that the food court was the most likely place with both quality space and outdoors access. He guided his bike towards it. He found the food court and some small shops nearby. He climbed off his bike and looked around.

"This could work," he said aloud. He climbed over an old door to look into what seemed like an old hat shop. It was dry, with a good temperature and good air. There also seemed to be decent foraging opportunities for food and supplies. Most importantly, he could set up a little air filter which would mean no more gas mask for awhile. Jon started unpacking his stuff from the bike and setting it outside the shop.

"I'll clear a space to cook and sleep tonight and then clean out the alcove tomorrow and see how it is." Jon took out his meat and made the walk over to the old restaurants. He looked around at the vents to the outdoors and looked at how best to make a smoker that wouldn't burn the place to the ground. He found some wooden furniture for fuel and using some pieces of sheet metal and a makeshift flue, in a matter of hours he had the deer smoking. Jon let the smoking continue as he fell onto his sleeping pad on the floor to get some much needed rest.

"Wake up! Wake the fuck up, you piece of shit!" Jon's eyes fluttered open. They were sticky. He held his hands up.

"No, No, I'm not sick, no threat." He tried to shout but his throat was dry and the words had less force than he wanted. His assailant poked him with the business end of a gun. He held his hands up higher.

"Get up, come on, get up!" The man with the gun grabbed his arm and pulled Jon into a standing position. Other men grabbed him and hauled him out. They quickly put a hood over his head and led him away.

"My stuff! My bike! Stop!" He shouted in vain. The men kept him walking. They kicked his legs to keep him moving. They marched on for several minutes until they finally stopped. He heard a door open and hushed voices. They kicked his knees out from under him and he collapsed into a chair. He felt a jab in the arm. It hurt for a moment. The bag was pulled off his face and his head darted around trying to see who had kidnapped him. His answer came with a slap to the face.

"Don't look around, fuck face." Jon shook his head and suppressed a cough. He swallowed but it was dry and it hurt a bit. They put the bag back on his head.

"My name is Jon, I'm not sick, I'm not trying to hurt you, just let me go. You'll never see me again."

"The King will determine what happens to you." Jon saw some light filter through the bag.

He heard a shuffling of feet and then silence. The small light had been turned off, plunging the room into darkness. "What's next?" he thought to himself. His answer came soon enough. He heard a door open and close. He felt the bag plucked away. His head swiveled around in the darkness. The small light came back on and Jon closed his eyes.

"Hello Jon - that's your name right?" Jon looked down to shield his eyes.

"Yes, why am I here? Who are you? Who is the King?"

"All in due time." Jon's eyes finally adjusted and he looked up at the man. "He seems friendly," Jon thought. He was tall with long legs. He wore boots and his pants were tight around his flat stomach. He flashed a broad smile of small teeth.

"Hi Jon, welcome. If you can talk calmly I can take off the ropes. But you have to promise me to behave like a good boy."

"Yes, I can do that." Jon felt uncomfortable in only his pants. His shoes and shirt had been taken away and he became conscious of his nudity.

"OK, great." The man moved behind Jon and loosened his ropes.

"What's your name?"

"What's that?"

"Your name. You never told me your name."

"I'm Brad," he said standing up again. He pulled over a metal chair. Jon turned his head to get a look at the room. There wasn't anything in it except the small light and the two chairs. This place had electricity and the room was in good shape and clean. The walls were white plaster and the floor was a low pile carpet.

"Hi Jon, I'm Brad, we covered that and now I'm sure you want to know what's going on."

"Yes, please," Jon said, rubbing his wrists and limbs.

"Our men found you on patrol this morning. And now, you have to go to the King for him to decide what should happen to you."

"Who is this Mr. King?"

"Oh no, not Mister, just King. King Christopher is kind. You've stumbled upon us here in the Kingdom of Nordstrom."

"What?"

"Here, I'll show you."

Brad stood up. "Come on, your claims are true, you aren't sick. I can show you around." Brad opened the door and let Jon out. They traveled down an area in the Mall. On the right was a checkpoint.

"I'm taking him on a tour," Brad told the guards. The men moved the barriers. The checkpoint was simple with a single booth made of various items and some rope barriers. Brad led Jon past the serious looking young men and towards the large entrance above which read "Nordstrom."

Jon kept walking past the chairs and other debris that surrounded the entrance.

"All this to keep people out?"

"Of course, King Christopher has created something special here. He saved us from the sick."

Jon started to survey what he could see. Rather than a department store full of racks and shelves he saw small houses. People stopped to look at him. Brad led him on.

"These are the dwellings that we have. Over here we have our downtown. See, the barber, the shops." He pointed at them. People with baskets stopped their trade to look at the newcomer. Jon looked around at them and they returned long stares. Jon kept walking.

"Come on, we're going to go see the farms." Away from the downtown area, Brad led Jon to large tanks of water and planters full of green things. Food grew in the planters.

"How is this possible?"

"The King created it. He sent out foraging parties for everything that we need."

"How does it all work?"

"The farms grow by putting nutrients in the water. The water is constantly recycled through the plants and back into the tanks."

"Air?"

"Filtered by filtration on the roof. That air pumps into almost the entire Mall."

"Power?"

"Static electricity rods on the roof. King Christopher mentioned someone named Tesla invented it."

"This King, what does he need from you to live here?"

"Loyalty, nothing besides loyalty. He created this as a sanctuary for survival. We're even starting to thrive. I'll show you our school."

Brad led Jon along the tanks until he turned left towards another street. They paused to look at a few buildings before arriving at a pavilion. Jon could hear kids talking and playing. "I don't even remember the last time I heard happy children," he thought to himself as he saw the kids playing on a playground of large plastic animals and soft ground.

"See, our kids are getting quality education. They had a field trip to the outside last week."

Jon looked around again. Brad tugged his arm. "Where did everyone come from?"

"Mostly they were here when the bombing happened. A few are like you, wanderers, but most never even saw their homes. They just created a new life here."

Jon looked over his shoulder at the children again. "These kids never knew the old world," Jon said.

"A few were young but no, this all they've ever known. Actually, my wife is pregnant right now, we're very happy." Brad stopped at another location after several few blocks.

"Here's our library. We've saved up some information, kept things, found things. In the beginning we were hoping for a connection to the outside world but we've been abandoned," Brad said, pointing at the building.

Jon looked at the people in the area, which was marked with a nice sign that said, "Library." It was open to the air and had low shelves as walls. People sat reading and small groups of children looked through some of the books.

"The rest have moved on. This area is abandoned, except for us and the little kingdom we've got going here." Brad put his hands in his pockets. "Maybe you can help us, brother."

Jon looked down again. "Help you? How?"

"Why don't we get your things and you can stay the night with me? Then you can decide if you want to join the kingdom and pledge your loyalty to the King."

Jon nodded. Brad started the trek through the village. Brad stopped at the checkpoint and sent one of the young men for Jon's clothes. The young man returned moments later. "Here, put these on, you'll need them." Jon dressed again. "That's much better," he said out loud.

Brad led him to the small area by the food court where he had camped. Jon picked up his stuff and looked around for his smoking operation.

"Where's my smoker?"

"We had that destroyed - we can't have any contaminants or smoke in the building."

"Shit. That was good deer meat."

Brad smiled. "Gather your things, we'll go eat. My wife is a great cook."

"Do you only eat plants?"

"And the fish that live in the tanks," Brad said, smiling at Jon. Jon piled all his stuff on the seat of his bike and started rolling it out. The men started back towards the kingdom.

"You'll have to leave the bike at the checkpoint. I'll help you carry your stuff." Brad and Jon arrived at the checkpoint and abandoned Jon's bike. They split the load and started in towards the village again. Brad wound through some streets and around other warm cottages made of all sorts of materials before stopping at a small door of a hut. The building was squat and was created from plastic pallets on the outside. Jon could see a metal frame.

"Honey, I'm home," Brad announced.

A thin woman, heavily pregnant, came to the door.

"Hello my love, I have dinner on."

Jon looked around the small cottage. He noticed the small mantle they had built around the radiator. The air around it was hot, he could see the waves of heat coming off the metal coils. Jon turned around to catch Brad and his wife kissing. Brad drifted his hand across her stomach. She pushed his hand away and started over towards the hearth. Brad took off his coat and hung it on a small hook by the door. Jon slipped out of his coat and took his gear down off his shoulders.

"Maryanne, meet Jon - he's a wanderer we found in the Mall today."

"I heard there was going to be a guest." Maryanne was squatting on the floor with a large spoon.

"This is the guest. I took him on a little tour."

"Has he seen the King yet?"

"No, that's tomorrow." Brad replied. Maryanne pulled out three small bowls and started ladling out soup from a large pot that was plugged in on the floor.

"What's in this?"

"It's just the town's forever soup."

"Oh, OK. What's in it?"

Maryanne smiled. "All sorts of things, fish, leeks, onions, cauliflower, and carrots, I think this is a fish broth too. Lots of good things and it's wonderfully warm." Maryanne handed Brad his bowl. Brad pulled out a chair at a small square table with a simple cloth over the top. Maryanne pulled her chair from the kitchen and towards the table. Jon looked around for a chair. Maryanne turned over a plastic carton. "Here's a cushion, I couldn't find another chair on such short notice. this'll have to do for now," she said with a smile.

Jon took the cushion and put it on the crate. Maryanne returned with two bowls. She set one before Jon and then placed her bowl in front of her. With a smile at Brad she started eating her soup. "Oh my! Bread!" She stood up and moved back to the kitchen. She pulled out a loaf of bread from a small cabinet and picked up a butter dish from the small counter and returned to the table. She pulled off the heel of the bread and handed it to Brad. He promptly dipped in the soup and took a big bite from the crust. Maryanne pulled of the next bit and handed it to Jon. She then removed another bit for herself. She gingerly spread some butter around the bread before eating it. Jon followed Brad's method. He dipped the bread in the soup and ate it. Everything tasted so real, almost like what food tasted like before the world went to shit and the air became poisoned. Jon cleaned his bowl and ate every crumb of bread offered.

"I haven't eaten like that since — well, since before."

Maryanne smiled, "I'm glad you like it." She stood up, holding her girth and moved back towards the kitchen. Jon held up a hand. "Mary, why don't you sit down in the corner and rest. I'll clean up the kitchen."

"And I will let you. My feet hurt terribly after today." Brad stood up and tugged at his pants. He picked up a bucket and poured some water and started to wash up the dishes. Jon leaned forward onto his knees and enjoyed the last of his tea in the domestic scene. Maryanne seated herself in a large pile of blankets and other soft material in the corner. She kicked off her shoes and let her body go limp for a moment.

"I'm ready for this baby to come," she declared out loud. "It's like someone made you swallow a big bag with a little man inside having a party."

"Or a little woman." Brad said with a smile over his shoulder as he poured out the dishwashing water.

"Brad is hoping for a girl and I'm hoping for a boy." Maryanne said with a smile. Jon smiled at her. "Beer?" Brad offered. Jon assented. Brad brought two small glasses of yellow liquid to the table and sat down next to Jon while Maryanne let her eyes close on her pad of softness. Jon looked around the cottage. It almost seemed normal.

Brad pulled out a soft blanket and laid it out. Jon dug through his pack for his sleeping pad and laid it out on the floor. Brad stood up and tried to move his wife so they would sleep in the little side bedroom. However, she waved him off and turned over on her side. Brad shrugged his shoulders and turned out the lights. He covered the fire and laid out in the small side bedroom. Jon looked into the blackness that was only broken by the gentle glow of the streets outside the cottage. He eventually fell off into sleep.

He woke up to the smells of cooking. He leaned up on his elbows and saw Maryanne rolling out some bread and stirring a pan.

"Good morning Jon. How are you?" Maryanne said.

"I'm alright, I guess. Do you guys have latrines?"

"Yes, we use a pot but you can visit the washroom. You can even shower if you want."

"A shower? Like a real shower?" Jon replied, sitting up.

"Yes! Brad? Would you take Jon for a shower?" Brad walked out of the small side room and rubbed his eyes.

"Sure, let me get my stuff." Brad picked up a small bag. Jon dug around for his soap from his pack.

"Let's go." Brad opened the door and led Jon out into the street and they started towards the bathrooms. The village was just coming to life. Brad waved at different villagers as they arrived at the large washroom. Brad led him to the men's side. There were four tubs against one wall, a bank of showers, and several toilets opposite.

"Do the toilets work?"

"They do, they compost and the waste goes into our water system. The waste makes a great compost, especially with our diet."

Jon walked into one of the stalls and sat down. He couldn't remember the last time he used a toilet like a real person. He relieved himself and joined Brad again. Brad picked a shower stall and turned on the water.

"You guys have hot water?"

"Of course, we use biomass heat and some electricity."

"Wow, I haven't had a hot shower in years." Jon stepped into the shower stall and took off his clothes. He turned on the water and started to wash his lean body. He let the hot water wash over him and he closed his eyes.

"Feel good, man?"

"It feels really good, like *really* good."

"Sometimes it's the little things," Brad said, shutting off the water.

Jon washed thoroughly before rinsing off. Brad waited for him as he dried off, using a small towel, and dressed again.

"Let's go have some breakfast and then we'll get you over to the King."

Brad started the walk back towards his cottage. Jon followed him over to it and the three people were soon enjoying their simple breakfast of fish, bread, cheese, and fruit.

Brad wiped his mouth on his sleeve. "Alright, we had better

start walking to see the King. I know he is eager to meet you."

He stood up and slung his small bag over his shoulder. Jon put his pack on his back. Brad leaned down to kiss his wife. She put a hand over her stomach. "Hurry home, love."

"I will."

The two men started out into the village, past open boxes of planters with flowers and food. Trees reaching up to the skylights covered their path and they made their way to the disused escalator. The pair climbed it and soon were upstairs. There were more cottages and huts and the space was buzzing with activity as people worked in open workshops on a variety of tasks. Jon saw women sewing, while others cut up food and put it in jars and still others were bashing metal or working on small parts and machines. Jon and Brad waved hello to some of the workers and kept going towards the back of the store.

Jon kept up with Brad easily. "So how did the king start this ...place?"

"I guess he used to work here, never got to go home or see his family. This is his home now." Brad replied. "It used to be a store and then he decided it was the place to survive. He took people in and created rules that we all live by for our mutual survival. As you can see, it's been successful. We're happy again."

They passed through two double doors where two young men stood.

"Hi, I have Jon here, he's here to see the king." The young men moved farther back. Jon surmised that at one time this was a stock room and now the private space for the King. The young man returned in a few moments and waved them into another part of the space. The open space of the stock room had been divided with pallets and other materials. The King sat on an old office chair near a desk. He stood up to greet them.

"So you are the traveler we've heard so much about?" The

King was a short Asian man. His hair was combed to one side. He held his hands in front of him.

"Yes, he stayed with us last night, we broke bread."

"Good, good. Thank you, Brad, for showing our guest hospitality. If you would wait outside while we talk."

Brad nodded his head and departed from the space.

"How are you enjoying our little refuge?" The King sat down on his chair again.

"I had a hot shower this morning for the first time in years," Jon said reaching his arms over his head.

The King nodded. "Yes, I think hot water is a nice thing to have, it's one of the first things we developed."

"It was great."

The King smiled. "Have you thought about joining our community?"

Jon looked down at his shoes. "I-I don't know, not really, I don't think."

"Ah, well as you can see, we've worked to create something sustainable here: we have a solid community that can continue on for a long time."

"I saw that," Jon said clasping his hands.

"Why don't you have a seat?" The King pulled out a simple metal framed chair, covered in grey cloth. Jon sat down on the chair and moved it closer to the King.

"Sustainability is our focus here. Whatever we do, it has to contribute to the ecology somehow. That includes people, too."

"I see."

"I really want to see if you could be a fit in our community." The King shuffled through some papers and found a small notebook. "Do you have any skills?"

"I can weld. I used to be a mechanic. I'm a hunter, that's how I survive, and I've gotten good at fixing things."

"I see. Are you a fast learner?"

"I think so." The King wrote that down. He wrote down other notes that Jon couldn't see.

"What kind of work did you do before the disaster?"

"I was a car mechanic mostly. I spent most of my time outdoors. Drank, partied with my friends and girls." The King kept writing.

"I see. Alright. Did you ever commit any crimes?"

Jon rubbed his hands. "I had a few interactions with the law, mostly traffic, I got a DUI one time when I was 22 but it was vacated, the cops screwed me over. I don't miss those guys."

"OK." The King noted that down.

Jon watched the King as he looked over his notes for several moments. The room was silent but the faint noise of the work outside could be heard through the wall.

"Jon, I'm going to be honest with you. We don't usually take in outsiders anymore. We've found it can be hard for some people to fit into the community and learn to live with our rules. We have to be strict so we can keep the community going. Everyone works on a task that builds the community. Whether that is farming or working in the workshops or running a store of goods, everyone has to work. We have community activities and fun too, but it is no easy thing to keep this place running and that's how we survive. We take crime very seriously. If someone steals something or tries to assault someone, we deal with that as a community and we decide how best to punish them and sometimes that means they are forced to leave. We give them some basic things to survive and wish them luck in the world but they can never come back."

"I see," Jon said, leaning into the chair. The chair was not comfortable and Jon shifted his body trying to find a better spot to sit.

"Also, breeding is important. We are the only people here, it is important that we form families and raise children. Currently, we have a few too many women and not enough men. I was just looking over the figures. Even my young soldiers are going to be fathers soon," the King said, pointing at some papers.

Jon smiled. "Does the King have a Queen yet?"

"Yes, my wife is pregnant now with our first heir."

"Yeah, I see the King has already done his job."

"Yes, we have many pregnant women in our community right now. It's an important part of being here. I'm sure you've seen a woman you'd like to be with already," the King said sitting back in his chair.

Jon chuckled. "I honestly hadn't thought about it. I haven't seen a woman in two years."

"Yes, well, it will come back to you. It's only natural."

"I guess, yeah it is," Jon said looking at the floor.

The King put down his pad of paper and leaned into his own chair. "I'd like to offer you a place here, if you want to stay. I can introduce you to some very nice women who are eager to contribute to the future of this community." The King shuffled through papers on his desk and looked a long list of names.

"I have a list of all the single women in our community. We can have some of them come in. You can see who you might like to talk to, who you find attractive."

Jon looked at him for a moment. "I-uh-I don't think that will be necessary." The King waved a hand. "Not at all, I'll show you." He picked up the phone and pressed a button.

"Yes, could you find Sarai, and have her come to my office? Yes, thank you."

"Sarai is young, she is only nineteen and she is eager. She is an important part of the garden downstairs."

"Oh-uh- OK." Jon looked over his shoulder.

"You'll see, she is very attractive. In another time, I think everyone in the kingdom would be trying to get with her, but we have strict rules around that. Family is very important to us."

The pair shared a silence that ended when one of the young soldiers appeared with Sarai next to him. She was dressed in a simple frock, her hair braided down her back.

"Did you need something?" she asked.

"Sarai, I want you to meet the traveler we found," the King said, standing. Jon stood up and shook her hand.

"Sarai, why don't you step out your dress for a moment." Sarai pulled her dress over her head to reveal her mostly naked body. A small bra covered her breasts. Jon looked at her and then looked away.

"It is no problem," the King reassured him. Sarai smiled.

"Thank you Sarai, you can dress." She slipped the frock over her head again. She stood facing the King. "Thank you, Sarai, you can return to work." Sarai smiled and bowed her head as she departed.

"Do all women do that?" Jon asked him.

"No, just for me, they understand," the King said. "Did you like Sarai?"

"I mean, yes, I-uh, yes, she was attractive, she was hot."

"I can see a very fruitful life for you here, Jon, if you want it."

"I don't know."

"Come with me for a moment." The King said standing up. They left the office and the King led them down the hall. He pointed through another door.

"This is our stock room, we keep all sorts of things here."

Jon moved through the door and into the stock room. The metal shelves were covered in pickled foods, pots, pans, and appliances. The shelves were labeled with their contents. The pair passed two women working at putting some things away. They had several papers that Jon presumed were lists of things in the store room.

"We try to save half of everything we make, grow, or create, that way we will always save it. We work at creating abundance in a world that is no longer what it was," the King said, walking through the aisles of stored food and items.

Jon looked at the tall shelves with all the goods and food again. He gawked at the amount of jars and wrapped things they had stored.

"I haven't seen this much food since before…" His voice trailed off as he looked at the stores.

The King held his hands behind his back. "See, we have everything you need."

Jon turned around in the warehouse. "Uh-yeah. Sorry I'm a little overwhelmed right now. Not sure what to think about all this."

The King laughed. "Come, let's let the ladies do their work here." The King led them through the maze of shelves back to his office. The King sat down in his chair and Jon sat down again too, rubbing his legs.

"What about leaving? Do you let people go outside?"

"Not usually, it's hard to leave. As you know, we have to clean ourselves and check ourselves for diseases every time we leave so I don't let people leave very often. So when you're here, you're here."

"I see, do I have to get naked all the time?"

The King laughed at the remark. "Not usually but there is a certain expectation of openness and obedience. If I walk up to you and I want to see your body, then compliance is usually required."

Jon rubbed his legs again. He took a deep breath. "I-I don't think I can join your, uh, collective here. I think I'd better go." Jon stood up and held out his hand. The King looked at it and did not shake back.

"That's very unfortunate, Jon, isn't it?"

"Yes," Jon said withdrawing his open hand.

"Yes, well, I can't force anyone to join us, especially if you already know the rules. But I don't think it's that. I don't think you trust me."

"I don't know about trust, it's just, I don't know, I like my freedom."

The King laughed out loud. "Your freedom to starve? Your freedom to die of a disease? Your freedom to be killed by an animal or someone else?"

Jon shrugged his thin shoulders. "Yeah, but I've survived this far."

"And how much longer will you survive?" the King said slipping out of his jacket. "How much longer can you forage, how much longer can you travel? What if you get hurt and there is no one to help you?"

Jon looked up at the ceiling. " I guess if my number is up, then my number is up." Jon shifted his weight between his feet. The King shook his head. "So fatalistic, but that is the time that we live in. Very well then. I'll have you escorted to the entrance where you can leave on your adventures. My only request is that you keep our location to yourself. We don't need an influx of sick people here."

Jon nodded his head. "I understand."

The King opened his hand to the door. "The soldiers will see you out." Jon opened the door and walked towards the soldiers. The King followed him as far as the double door entrance.

"Escort Jon to his motorbike at once please," the King directed. Brad stood up when he saw Jon appear outside the double doors. Brad gave him a broad smile. "What did you decide?"

"I'm leaving, right now apparently."

Brad's countenance fell. "I'm sorry to hear that. I really thought you'd enjoy living here."

Jon tilted his head. "It's not a problem, I've survived this far and I'll continue surviving. I'll find somewhere to stay that's safe."

Brad shook his head. "What if—" Jon interrupted him. "I don't live in what ifs. I live in what I know and what it takes to make it. I'll make it. Enjoy becoming a father." Jon started his walk downstairs to the main entrance. Brad followed him just before the sealed entrance. Jon looked back at Brad one more time. He thought about Sarai, he thought about what he had seen. He took two deep breaths and crossed the barrier back out into the disused Mall. His bike was sitting there with his side saddles attached. He shifted his pack and climbed aboard. He kicked away from the floor and rode out of the Mall and back outside into the air. He put his gas mask on and started riding away from the Kingdom.

America Discount World

The gentle waters of Lake Union lapped against the edge of his large house boat. He rolled off his sturdy foam mattress and stood up. He draped a robe around his body and scratched his hairy belly, then tugged at the tight trunk underwear that covered him. He poked his head out of the patio door for a moment. The puffy grey clouds passed by over his nearly bald head. Dale stretched a bit, slipped off his robe and started to perform some calisthenics on the small patio. The patio just fit his compact 5' 8" frame as he performed a series of pushups. In fifteen minutes he stood back up and looked at the sky again.

"Just a break in between the rain," he said aloud. He clenched his eyes shut and shut the patio door, then pulled the long white curtains over the big glass doors.

"Fantastic, I need to figure out what's going on today. Another day, another yuan or dollar or euro," he said out loud. He rubbed his head and sauntered towards the bathroom, emerging a few minutes later with wet hair and a towel around his waist. His small belly drooped over the towel a bit. He made his way down a narrow stairway to the first level of the house boat and sat at the kitchen counter on a high chair. He poured himself some cold cereal and hemp milk.

"Hey Anna, what's on my calendar today?"

"Good morning Dale," the small blue pill-like device replied.

Dale kept chewing.

"What do I have to do today?"

"You have a couple of appointments," she said in a cheery but synthetic voice. "Your first appointment is at 10:45 A.M. Meet buyer at storage unit in Belltown."

"Fuck. What time is it, Anna?"

"It's 9:45 a.m. Dale."

"How long will it take me to get from Home to Vine St. Storage?"

"Traffic is moderate right now, it will take you forty minutes to get to Vine St. Storage from here."

"Fuck it, I'll eat in the car." Dale set the bowl down and went back upstairs. He pulled on a pair of black jeans and a black t-shirt. He covered his shoulders with a black jacket and slipped into some thick leather boots. He stepped over clothes, a few boxes and some plastic bags to get back to the door.

He pulled out a small black bag, checked for his device, his car fob, and his house fob and then returned downstairs. He picked up his bowl of cereal and started out to his car. He was about to close the door behind him when he felt a furry familiar brush his leg.

"Are you actually going to come in, Legolas?"

The grey striped cat poked his round face around the door and licked a paw before disappearing into the house boat.

"I'll take that as a yes." Dale went back inside and put down a bowl of water for his part-time cat. "I think this bowl of dry food is still OK," Dale said as he put it down in the white tray on the floor. Dale took a few bites of his cereal and watched Legolas circle his way toward the food and water. Dale sipped the milk out of the bowl as the cat nibbled away.

"Fuck, I need to go. Don't tear the place up," Dale said to the cat. Legolas looked at him and turned his head back and forth. He crouched down and closed his eyes.

"Alright then." Legolas opened his eyes again and started licking his fur. "I'm off. See you when I see you." Dale walked out to his car and unplugged it from the charging post at the end of his slip. He opened the front door and sat down. He pushed a large grey button and the car lit to life. The center screen greeted him in simple blue letters, "Hello Dale."

"Hey Anna, let's get going to Vine Street Storage and I'd like to hear the latest headlines on the way."

"It's forty seven minutes to Vine Street Storage. Beginning route." The car began to move backwards. It pulled out of the little scrap of pavement on which Dale parked the car near his dock and moved out of the Marina and towards the city.

"The news from Reuters and AP-CNN," Anna announced.

"Today President Ivanka Trump announced a new trade policy with Indonesia. It's widely seen as progress as Asia seeks new trading partners outside of the new Silk Road."

"Popular singer Ariana Grande has died in her home in New Zealand, she was 55. Tributes are pouring in all around the world."

"Google has announced updates to its popular self-driving automobile software. This is in response to a recent hacking scandal where millions were unable to leave their homes."

"Today is Elon Musks' birthday, the prominent inventor would have been 77 today."

"That's the North American headlines for June 28, 2048."
Dale thumbed on his tablet.

"Anna, play some jazz, and turn on an overhead light." A soft light illuminated his head and jazz began playing.

The car glided through traffic and circled around the block until it finally stopped at his storage building on Vine Street. "Thanks, Anna."

"Will you be loading or unloading?" Anna asked.

"Yes, both. I'll be back in a few minutes."

Anna opened the rear hatch. It slowly opened. Dale looked at his device and took out three bins from the back of the car. He set these on the ground and looked over his shopping list. "I have a good idea of where most of this is but a couple of these, I'll need to go find," he said out loud to himself. He walked down the concrete hallway of Vine Street Storage. He made his way around to one of his three units on the block. Dale unlocked all three storage units and started shopping.

The storage units were filled with special objects, all neatly displayed on large shelves he had built within the storage units. Complete series of books like Harry Potter, Eragon, and others filled plastic bags. Early electronics also sat on small stands, neatly displayed and ready for sale. Small framed drawings dominated another shelf. Stacks of DVD cases lined another wall. Then there was the storage locker filled from floor to ceiling with computer game disks, vinyl records, and VHS tapes. Dale walked into the first unit and found the small safe in the back that held the keys.

"First I need the keys for the 69 Mustang so I can start the permit process of getting it moved." He tapped on his device as he pocketed the small keys to the classic car. Dale used battery powered lights to illuminate the industrial spaces. "A complete set of 50 Shades of Grey in leather. I think that's in Unit 2. Oh and here's one I need to find. An original Macbook Air. That's probably over with the other Apple stuff. I'll look for it while I'm packing up that iPhone 4s." Dale kept talking as he filled the plastic bins with all the objects, neatly packed in brown paper and boxes, beginning to make their way from his storage unit to their new homes around the world.

Dale's phone buzzed. He looked at the message. It read simply. "Here." Dale plucked up three piece of art wrapped in paper that he laid against the door of Unit 1. "On my way," he texted back. Dale walked out of the storage center and looked around. A tall guy wearing a long jacket waved a brown hand at him.

"Dale?" His South Asian accent was strong.

"Yeah."

"Alright, you got the drawings?"

"Of course." Dale handed them over. He took them and gingerly opened the back of one. He looked at the surface and smiled. He opened the others and nodded, taping them back shut.

"Alright, let me send the rest of the money."

Dale held up his phone and waited for the transaction. "Perfect." Dale said when the transaction had completed itself. "Great, a pleasure, man. Have a great day."

Dale waved at him as he stepped into a car service. Dale walked back into the storage unit and got back to work. Over an hour had passed before he finally packed everything up and started to close all the doors on his work spaces. Dale had closed the final door when he turned around and saw a short woman, not more than thirty five with a neat bob haircut, standing in the hallway. Dale tried to ignore her but she spoke first.

"Hey there."

"Hi," Dale said back quietly.

"Uh, could you help me out a bit?"

Dale turned around and set down his bins. "I'm in a hurry, sort of."

"It's just a minute, I — I just divorced my husband and all my stuff is behind his stupid dining room table. I was hoping you could help me. Can you help me move his table out so I can get to my stuff?

Dale sighed. "What if you slide the boxes over the table to me and I put them out here, then you can get a wagon to move them out of here."

"That's a great idea! Would you? I—I can pay you a little. My name is Jenna." She held out her hand to shake his.

Dale took off his jacket. "No charge, let's just get busy. I do have to get going."

She unlocked her door and swung the door outward. "Just picking up some stuff yourself?" she said.

"Dear God, she wants conversation!" Dale thought to himself. "Yeah, you know."

"What do you do?" she said, scooting around the oval table towards a pile of boxes in the back. She started to shift several boxes.

"I'm a broker."

"Oh cool, houses?" she said pulling a plain brown box from the pile in the back of the locker.

"Cultural goods," Dale said as he took the first box and stacked it in the hallway.

"Oh that's cool, I didn't know there was a market for that." She slid another box across the table.

Dale kept neatly stacking the boxes outside in the hall. After 25 boxes had passed, she said, "Finally, I'm out of his life. I can move on." She held her arms in the air in victory, then shut the door behind her. "Thank you so very much, you've made a really bad day a little bit better. I'm grateful."

"You're welcome."

"Can you tell me more about what you broker? I didn't know Seattle had a market for cultural artifacts."

"We're selling off every little bit of American culture we've got. It's worse than what happened in Europe after WWII."

"Who's the buyers?"

"Mostly Arabs, Chinese, Indonesian more now, India, lots of India, and sometimes South American, mostly Brazilian too."

"What do they buy?"

"A lot of books, I have a Chinese collector of John Grisham.

I never thought that would be in-demand in the book market. But it's also old fast food promotional signs. Funko pops are popular if they are in good condition."

"So listen, I'm a writer at the Seattle Stranger-Times and I think this could be an interesting article. "America: Now for Sale.""

Dale picked up his bins. "I'm not one for attention, especially in the press."

"You could stay anonymous. I think this is really fascinating. Someone is just selling off the early 21st century, just like that," she said eagerly.

"Alright, I guess, maybe that could work. It might be interesting. OK, sure, I'll talk to you."

"Great! Uh, let's exchange contact info. I'll message you with a day and a time and we'll meet up!"

"Sounds great," Dale said turning to leave. Jenna smiled and waved at him as she headed in the opposite direction. Dale used his device to summon his car and loaded the back with the bins and directed the car to return him to his houseboat. As his car pulled into the Marina he received a message from Jenna. "Thursday, at 2 p.m. Do you have a preferred meeting place?" the message read. Dale sent her his location. "You can come to my home," he typed back. He sat down in his lounger and tapped away on his phone. He scheduled a pickup for the packages from his device and got busy sending out follow-up invoices for his objets d'art. He connected his label printer and put labels on all his boxes.

"Anna, put, package pickup, tomorrow at 11 am on my calendar."

"Adding package pickup tomorrow at 11 am to your calendar," the blue pill device replied.

"Thank you."

"You're welcome, Dale. Would you like to hear a joke?"

"Not right now."

"OK."

Jenna arrived at the appointed hour. Her taxi pulled up at the slip right at two. Dale opened the big sliding door that led out to the driveway.

"Hi Dale!" Jenna wore a simple suit and a practical jacket. Dale wiped his hands on his pants before extending his hands.

"Welcome to the lake," Dale said, motioning her indoors. Jenna took in the houseboat before following him in. Dale sunk into his big lounger and she sat on a divan opposite him. A low table held some glasses and a pitcher of tea. The houseboat was neat. Dale had cleaned up the pile of dishes and had sorted the place out. It looked simple, masculine, and ready to receive visitors. She set out her device. "Recording." Dale nodded before knocking back his glass of bourbon.

"Drink?"

"Tea, please."

"Alright."

Dale handed her a glass bottle of tea. She opened it easily and set it down.

"So what do you want to know about the antique business?"

"I thought you were a cultural broker."

"Same thing."

"Ah, OK." She noted that down and took a big gulp of the tea.

"How did you get into being a cultural broker?" She leaned in towards him to hear the answer. Dale leaned back and looked out a small window. "I've been selling shit since college."

"What did you sell?"

"Text books, if you can believe it - paper textbooks were huge back then. They were so expensive and everyone was trying to save a buck. That started my addiction to selling stuff. Then, when the trade wars broke out stuff started to come around cheap and I started to buy stuff up for myself. It started as stuff that I liked and wanted to keep around. But I was still re-selling stuff online because I could get multiples of it. So I would buy three of something and then sell the other two to pay for the one I wanted for myself. Then it became a business, mostly word of mouth." Dale leaned forward in the lounger.

"What did you do before you started selling these things?"

"I worked in tech, random jobs, marketing, media. I'm an artist so I know how to survive. When things got bad in the economy and things really got crazy, I had to survive and selling off stuff to overseas buyers was a way to do that. My parents' generation bought shit, Jenna, they bought a lot of it, they had the money you know? They had all those good jobs and so when they died people inherited these houses full of crap and so you could go around to different neighborhoods and get furniture, newspapers, books, DVDs, for nothing and resell them to somebody in China."

"How do you decide what's valuable and what's just junk?" She held up her hands ready for an answer.

"I listen to my buyers and sometimes I just have a sense about things. American culture has been the cultural icon for awhile. And now it's on sale. You can get art, books, cars, alcohol, tech, signage, anything. It probably should go into museums for everyone, but like in the past, it's ending up in private collections. Hopefully it will get out again, maybe someday."

"I think people will find it hard to believe that Chinese people want hardback books." Jenna said, "In this day and age, who has time for paper?"

"You would be surprised. For example." Dale stood up and walked over to a bookcase. "This is a copy of the Divergent series, it's like from 2010 or something. Huge demand. At least it's not ending up in the garbage. Oh and objects get folks excited too. Especially old tech. I can't keep old Apple products in stock."

"Who knew that stuff would ever be valuable?" Jenna said, inspecting the books. Dale opened a drawer and took out a small rectangle of metal and glass. "This is an original iPod Touch. I keep this for my own nostalgia, but I could sell this for around $50,000, especially because it works." Dale demonstrated by turning the device on. The screen blinked to life revealed the small icons across the screen and the familiar Apple logo. Jenna snapped a picture of it.

"What about art like paintings and stuff? Do you do much in that?" Jenna said.

"I don't do too much art. That's a completely different market. Different museums sell off stuff to keep their doors open. They have that market pretty well sewn up. Sometimes I will sell pieces of lesser American artists. Many of my customers just want an American artist in their home so they will settle for prints, even well preserved posters can sometimes be a mover when the right person is interested. I do get a lot of requests for anime art."

"What's the most expensive print or poster you've sold?"

Dale chuckled as he put the small electronic device back in its box and back in the drawer. "Honestly?"

"Yes."

"A Nicki Minaj album cover. Just a poster of it but it was signed original from 2017 or 18, maybe 2019. Somewhere late decade. Anyway, yeah, I know a collector."

"Wow. I don't think most folks even know who she is anymore," Jenna said. "And isn't she like her in 60s or something?"

"Yeah, you had to have been there for that," Dale said, returning to his seat by Jenna.

Jenna wrote down more notes on her tablet. "Very interesting. You said the buyers were mostly Asian?"

"Yes, a few African. The Chinese have cooled down for obvious reasons, their country is having some issues, but I ship globally. Arabs. I guess everyone is looking for something that they don't have."

"Do you think we peaked?" Jenna said, looking up from her notes.

"Peaked?" Dale said, pouring out more tea. "Do you think we have peaked?" Jenna asked.

"I think once you started thinking like that, it probably means you have." Jenna wrote down the statement carefully.

She looked up at him. "This has been interesting. I think we've got something here. Is there anything in your private collection you could never part with?"

Dale chuckled, "There's not much, I'm mostly for sale. Let's see. I have a Marcel DuChamp print from a friend. I have some really great heirloom jewelry and one of my sets of china is pretty close to me so I would never sell those."

"For any price?"

"I'm not so stupid to think there isn't a price. Everyone has a price, it depends on the value of the object to the collector."

Jenna laughed. "What are you drinking?"

"Bourbon and tea. I was just about to get myself one, interested?"

"Special bourbon?"

"Not really, but I have some select bottles of authentic Irish whiskeys and some Scotches as well. There isn't a huge market for that. The market for wine is still larger. Wine is meant to be old."

"Can I have some?" Jenna said, holding out her glass. Dale stood up and brought the decanter over from his bar and poured out some liquid in her glass. She added the tea on top.

"So why do you think people obsess over American cultural objets d'art?" Jenna said after sipping some of the smooth copper liquid.

Dale stretched out. "You're too young to remember. Overseas, when I was your age, American everything was a must-have. Chinese tourists used to be decked out in Polo and other American and European brands. TV, movies, everything was American. We were a cultural powerhouse. For a certain generation, our cultural detrius still has collectable power as art. I think it's a way to remember things the way they used to be. It's all a pleasant memory of a simpler time." Dale swirled his drink. "We do live in a boring dystopia, after all."

Jenna sniffed the liquid, "This is really good."

"Yeah?" he replied.

"Ah, day drinking, always tastes better."

Dale laughed. "Always, always." He took a large sip and sat back down near her. Legolas appeared and stared intently at Jenna.

"Here kitty kitty." She beckoned.

"He probably won't come over, he's not even really my cat, he just sort of showed up one day. I put out a litter box, but he never uses it, which is cool, I guess, and he comes and goes."

"Aw, I was hoping he'd come over." Legolas sat down and kept a watchful eye on Jenna. He licked a paw but never broke his gaze.

"So why do you think we live in a boring dystopia?" Jenna asked. She set her drink down and prepared to take more notes.

"Eh, look around, nothing is pretty anymore, it's all just functional. Everything is white, clean and boring, there's no beauty, there's no frivolity, it's just useful, everything and everyone only has value if its useful, it's like we all live in the world of Thomas the Tank Engine and we're all trying to be Really Useful."

Jenna tilted her head. "Thomas the what?" she asked.

"It's an old children's show, that's my generation, go look it up later, you'll see."

Jenna made a note. She drank more of the bourbon tea again. "That's good."

"Hows that divorce coming along?" Dale asked. He gazed out the window and let the question hang in the air. Jenna took a deep breath before she replied. "It's, well, it's, going along I guess, but we're not talking about my divorce, we're talking about you." She redirected. "Married? Children?"

"Divorced, one kid, doesn't talk to me much. He's a climate adaptability engineer, he helps cities and countries deal with climate change."

"Bad divorce?" Jenna said, drinking more of her drink. She set the glass back down as he answered.

"Yeah, it was messy, it's actually how I ended up here on Lake Union. She got the house and my friend owned this and wasn't using it so I just moved in here and then he wanted to sell so I bought it off him and so I just have to make sure I don't sink."

Jenna looked around the houseboat. She leaned over to catch a glimpse of the kitchen and the obviously Ikea-made cabinets. She looked around at the Ikea-chic furniture.

"You shop at Ikea?"

"All the time, good stuff, cheap, it's just me now and it's light, don't want to be over weight, remember, I can't sink."

"Right, don't want to put too much on the boat."

"Exactly, more bourbon?"

"Sure." Jenna finished her drink and handed him back the glass. Dale sat down and made up two new drinks. He emptied the bottle of tea.

"I'll tell you what went wrong with mine if you tell me what went wrong with yours," Dale offered.

"You first," Jenna said.

"Alright, we got married in our early thirties, we hadn't been together very long. At that age, you don't…" He fell silent for a moment. "Want to waste time. Most of our friends had already gotten married and had kids so we wanted to catch up. We started dating and six months later got married. Three months after that our son was on the way." Dale drank from his glass. "Everything seemed fine but having kids changes you, it changes your relationship."

"It does, and if you can't have kids, that also changes things." Jenna looked out onto the water. The sun was getting lower in the sky. The glittering towers, looking small in the distance, reflected the light. Jenna held her tablet in her lap. Her electronic pencil was placed behind her ear as she sat back in the chair for a moment.

"Yes it does," Dale said. "And that's when the fights started. We hadn't really talked about how to raise a kid together and what we wanted. She was very strict, I wasn't. She felt like I was undercutting her. She didn't like being the bad parent." Dale used air quotes when he said *bad parent.*

"A classic."

"Yeah, Then everything seemed to be a proxy for that. I thought she should go back to work because her career was so important to her and we needed the money anyway. She wanted to stay home and just be a mom."

"Been there, done that." Jenna laughed, drinking more of the concoction.

"Yeah, so cue years of fighting and after fifteen years we finally agreed it wasn't working and we didn't want to do it anymore. It sucked for my son, by that time he was in highschool and I moved out. It sucked, he just showed up from school one day and I was gone. He never forgave me for that stunt."

"Yeah, I can see why you guys don't talk." Jenna said.

"Alright, your turn," Dale said. "Besides, what more can I tell you about the stuff I sell? Other than don't bother trying to sell

Lenox stuff, no one wants it, and old jewelry, sell it for the gold and stones. Oh and I always need old writing utensils, especially fountain pens, who knew they would ever be hot, right?"

"Fountain pens? Really? In this day and age?"

"You'd be surprised at what people buy."

"Well." Jenna turned off recording. "I met Adi in college, we were college sweethearts, dated all through college and for some reason it worked but when we graduated, things didn't work so well. But we got married anyway. I was just starting out as a journalist and he was working in social media."

"Not that Facebook/Amazon monstrosity?"

"Yup, and it is a mess, and it turned him into a mess, especially after the Baidu buyout."

"Stress all around?"

"Yeah, so we worked a lot, hung out in the evenings and then tried to have kids. I miscarried three times and every time he took it personally, like really personally. He thought it was his fault, it really brought out his insecurities, as a man I think. I tried to take the blame, I explained to him it was my body that wasn't cooperating, he did his job, we were making babies, I just—" Her voice stopped short of the sentence.

"Nature wasn't so keen on the idea?"

"My body just wasn't cooperating with our plans and it just hit all the problems with our relationship we had overlooked, things we hadn't resolved and then one day I came home, his stuff was gone and I got a letter from his lawyer with papers." She bit her lip. "I made it easy, I signed, it was over pretty quick and then I had to pick up my stuff, you saw that."

"Damn. Damn. Why are relationships so hard?"

"I don't know, I really don't," Jenna said wiping a tear away from her eye. " I guess it's a good thing I didn't bother with eyeliner today!" she added, forcing a laugh.

The sun started to disappear. Dale stood up and opened the

sliding door. "Come look at this, its beautiful, everyday it's clear." Jenna stood up and looked out to the water. The sunlight danced across the lake. Small boats were motoring into the marina after a day on the lake. The hum of their motors filled the silence between the two.

"Probably not what you thought today was going to be about, eh?" Dale said, breaking the silence.

"It wasn't in my story plan," Jenna said flatly.

"Would you like something to eat? I can order something for us."

"That would be lovely." Jenna touched Dale's arm for a lingering moment. Dale reached over and rubbed her arm to reassure her. He leaned against the railing for a moment before he took out his phone and started to scroll. "What kind of food?"

"Anything, teriyaki, sushi, all fine."

"Great, there's a great place called Marina Sushi, it's just down here. I'll order it up." Dale tapped the screen several times.

"Ten minutes, let me get some plates." Dale turned to go inside and Jenna followed him. She sat down and watched him get out plates and set the small table near the kitchen. He cleared some papers and other personal items from the table and wiped it down. He put out a little vase. He took a moment to put on a sports commentary program on the TV but the volume was very low. The subtitles flashed across the screen. Footsteps on the dock let Dale know that the food was here. Dale grabbed the large sack of food from the guy outside. He unpacked the meal and set it out on the table.

"Dinner is served," Dale announced with a sweep of his hand.

Jenna stood up and walked over to the two chairs around the small table. "That looks good." Dale moved to the wine cooler in the kitchen. "I forgot the wine." He popped the cork and returned with two stemmed glasses.

"Just let it air for a minute, we won't bother with decanting it." Jenna smiled. "You're–just–this is amazing, people don't live like this anymore."

"Wine from a bag just doesn't compare," Dale said pouring out the wine into their glasses. He swirled it around and smelt it a few times before finally tasting the golden liquid.

"That's good."

Jenna used the chop sticks to gather pieces of sushi from each of the rolls. The pair focused on eating. Jenna tried the wine. "It is very good, it's light, not too sweet, it actually tastes good."

"Told you, bag wine is overrated."

"It really is, and in real glasses too, that's impressive. You're impressive." Jenna reached over and took his hand. Dale smiled and put his hand on top.

"Thanks, no one really has ever said that before."

Jenna took her hand and continued eating. Soon all the sushi had disappeared and the bottle of wine was empty. Dale leaned back.

"That was good, good suggestion. The tuna roll was fresh."

"It was."

"I imagine you'll want to get back," Dale said with a smirk.

"To an empty micro apartment? Not really. I thought about getting a cat."

"Get one that sticks around unlike Legolas."

"Yeah, where is he?"

Dale shrugged his shoulders. "Probably left when we opened the door. He might be back. He might not."

Jenna stood up and smoothed her outfit. She gathered her things and put them in her bag. She stood by the door to the pier. Dale stood near her. "Thanks for coming, I'll have to look for the story."

"Yeah, I'll let you know." Jenna lingered for a moment. Dale offered his hand. Jenna shook it and pulled him close to her body.

"I haven't been with anyone since the divorce."

"Been with—"

"Sexually." She cut him off with a word.

"Oh, ah, aren't I a little old?"

Jenna replied with a kiss. Dale opened his lips and the kiss deepened. Jenna dropped her bag. Dale broke away to take off his shirt and they kept kissing. Dale led her towards the bedroom. Jenna let her clothes fall as they went. The pair flopped down on the simple mattress and sheets. Dale laid on the bed and Jenna straddled him exploring his body with her mouth. Dale's hands roamed over her curves. She loosed her bra revealing her breasts. Dale sat up to enjoy them. She wrapped her arms around him and held him close.

The pair reached an excitable but loving moment of ecstasy, trading positions and enjoying the full body skin contact. Jenna rolled out of bed first.

"Do you have a cigarette?"

"Yeah, I have a pack I keep for those rare occasions when I want to smoke."

"Can I have one?"

"Always." Dale stood up and slipped on some loose pants. He walked out of the bedroom and Jenna followed him gathering her clothes. He offered a cigarette and a light. Night had enveloped the marina and the city lights were the only source of outside illumination. The houseboat was dark. Dale put on a light and Jenna found her bag.

"I-I better order a taxi. Bathroom?" Dale pointed. Jenna disappeared for a moment. Dale listened for the toilet flush and presented her with a glass of water when she reappeared.

"Thanks, I'm thirsty." Jenna polished off the glass in a couple of swigs.

"Thank you, that was pretty great."

"You too, you're, uh, better than the ex and bigger too."

"My ego appreciates it." Dale said laughing.

Jenna felt her pocket vibrate and she looked at her device. "That's me."

"I'll walk you out." Dale walked with her to the end of the pier. The night air was chilly and Dale regretted not putting on a shirt. He saw Jenna into her taxi and the car pulled away silently. Dale stood on the pier for a moment before retreating into the warmth of the houseboat. He poured another bourbon.

"Anna, put on some music."

"From your favorites, this is Money Grabber by Fitz and the Tantrums."

Dale sipped his bourbon and looked out the window in contemplation. "That wasn't a boring dystopia day," he said out loud. He heard a clawing at the sliding door. He looked at Legolas through the glass. "You want to come in?" Legolas pawed the door again. "Alright." He opened the door and Legolas came in and curled up in a corner, tucking his legs under his body and slowly closing his eyes.

The Classy Drug Dealer

Andrej leaned against the large washing machine and browsed his magazine. He wore a neatly ironed shirt tucked into slim fitting slacks. The broad collar of the shirt stood open. He flipped through the pages and looked around the large laundromat, shifting in his leather loafers.

Four rows of washers and four banks of dryers lined the airy space. Metal exhaust pipes for the dryers dominated the tall ceilings. Behind the counter, a register and card machine stood, well worn. A large automatic clothing rack filled with clothes neatly draped in thin plastic filled the space behind. From the counter, customers could see the large orange dry cleaning machines with the colored tubes and hoses sprouting out of the side of them.

Large fans were posted around the room to keep the air moving. The glass and steel door was propped open for air. The floor was covered in aging linoleum that at one time was probably cream colored, but now was a mixture of cream and brown. Large rubber-backed rugs covered the area around the door and the counter. The gentle hum of machines running filled the air. Andrej looked over at the counter near the door. Baskets of laundry stood on the counter with more bags behind near the large conveyor. Outside the building a simple sign announced the business within, "Laundromat and Dry Cleaning." The top of the windows were painted with different services. "Wash and Fold" "Shirt Laundry" and "Coin Laundry."

"Hey, do you make change?" an old woman asked. She smacked her lips with her words. Andrej looked from his magazine. He wordlessly pointed at the 70s style, brown change machine in the corner. She nodded and tottered over to the machine. A small Asian lady came around the corner carrying cleaning supplies.

"Mama san, did you put in that batch?"

"Ya, ya, it going now." Andrej nodded. "Thanks Mama." He put down his magazine when he saw a customer come into the shop.

"Yeah, I'm here to pick up, three shirts and two pairs of pants." The man was slim, professional, and had a prominent adam's apple. His face sported an uneven beard which added a human element to his bland uniform slacks and collared shirt.

"Do you have your ticket?"

The man handed over the slip of paper. Andrej found his number and the clothes. He pushed the ticket down onto his spindle of tickets. He pressed a green button and the machine came to life with clothes flying by until Andrej came to the number he was looking for. He took the clothes off the rack and took them over to the plastic roll. He pulled a packet from his pocket and slipped the bag into the shirt hanger. He pulled plastic over the garments and took them out to the man. He put them on the hook. The man laid out his credit card and some cash. Andrej ran his credit card for the cleaning and pocketed the cash in a deft motion across the counter. The man was stony faced as he picked his card and shoved his wallet into his pants.

"Pleasure as always." Andrej looked through the door as he left with the clothes and a brief wave.

Andrej returned to his magazine. He looked up at the clock. "Two hours," he thought to himself. The sign outside clearly said last load had to be in by 8 p.m. The old lady carefully took her clothes out of the washer and put them in the dryer. She returned to her chair and stared up at the TV in an almost trance like state. Andrej finished his magazine just in time to feel his phone vibrate. The text was from a regular number. The kid was young, no more than twenty or twenty one. The kid was a good customer and looked like a parody of a gang banger. Andrej read the text.

"Hey I'm dropping by later."

"No problem," Andrej replied.

"Great." Andrej scrolled through his phone looking at other messages. The clock came up to 7 p.m. and Andrej was busy getting people's dry cleaning back to them. Several customers passed through the laundromat. Andrej separated the clothes with blue and pink tags. Pink tags were regular customers. Blue tags were special customers. Those customers had their choice of pills carefully left in the pocket of the garment or in the clothes hanger paper. They paid with cash and card. Card for the cleaning and cash for the pills. Andrej repeated the process just like before for ten customers in a row. Eight blue tags, two pink tags. Andrej checked the big orange washing machines to see which ones were done. He started to remove the clothes from the machines and got them ready for steaming and finishing. He opened all four machines and unloaded them. Mama san came around the corner.

"All done Mama?"

"Ya, ya, all done, I see tomorrow."

"Alright Mama san, see you tomorrow." Andrej hung up several clothes to get them ready for finishing. He removed the thick wad of cash from his pocket and knelt down at the desk. He tucked the money away in a little spot under the register to retrieve later. He looked around the laundromat to see if that older lady had left. The dryers were all quiet and the washers were all silent. Andrej walked around opening all the washer doors. He saw the clock was at 7:45, and mentally prepared to close. He saw four fresh baskets of clothes that Mamasan had finished and took them behind the counter for pickup. A moment later a man walked in. Rain had started to pelt down on the broken sidewalk outside the laundry. The water streaked down the glass as the rain picked up. Andrej noticed the man's square jaw. His mind turned over the possibility that the man was a cop. Andrej kept his cool. The man shook his shoulders from the wet as he walked in.

"Dropping off?" Andrej asked.

The man looked him straight in the eyes. "Are you Andrej?"

"Yes?"

The man pulled out a gun from his coat in a swift but smooth motion. "Close up," he ordered. Andrej's hands flew up.

"Do—do you want the register? I can open it for you, just don't fucking shoot!"

"No, I don't need your filthy money, just close up your shop." He waved the gun towards the door. Andrej walked out from behind the counter and turned the sign around from open to closed and lowered the black shades to obscure the view inside the shop. He turned off half the lights in the shop.

"There, closed up for the night," Andrej announced putting his hands back up.

"Over there, sit down, we need to talk." Andrej didn't move. "I don't know you, I can't help you. I can give you some money, if you're hard up, but I don't know what you want."

"Sit down, asshole." Andrej slowly obeyed the gunman, who revealed his face in the shadowy light. He wore a rain jacket and simple jeans; his face was older, his hair salt and pepper and the smile lines obvious. He was fairly fit from what Andrej could see under his jacket. He wasn't tall, they were similar in height, just under six foot. Andrej settled into one of the plastic chairs. The man kept the gun pointed at Andrej as he pulled another chair around.

"I know what you do."

"I own a laundromat, man, I don't know what you've heard." Andrej did not make eye contact with him. He looked away from the gunman.

"And you use it as a front for selling pills."

"Bullshit," Andrej replied.

The man took out a large smartphone. He swiped through some pics with his free hand.

"You recognize this kid?"

Andrej looked at the picture of the kid. He wore a nice polo shirt, short blonde hair, and blonde facial hair. He was smiling in the photo.

"Yeah, I recognize him but I never seen him in those clothes."

The gunman put his phone away. He stuffed his free hand in his jacket pocket. He pointed the gun around the room. "You buy all this with your drug money?"

Andrej held up his hands again. "I don't know what you're talking about man, you're crazy. Look, if you just fucking leave I won't call the cops, you on something?"

The gunman laughed. He threw his head back. "No, you fucking piece of trash. I'll tell you why I'm here. You piece of shit. I'm here because of my son."

"That your son?"

"Yeah."

"He came in a few times to get some stuff cleaned. He texted me earlier, he's probably coming in any time, you don't really want him to see you here holding me up, yeah?"

The gunman pulled the slide back on the gun and chambered a round with a loud click that echoed in the space.

"Trust me, he won't be coming here or anywhere ever again."

"What?" The gunman reached across the empty space between them and used the pistol grip of the gun to strike Andrej across the face. Andrej leaned over in his chair cursing. The gunman sat back down as Andrej held the right side of his face. When he moved his hand he could feel a nasty bruise developing and his teeth were stained with blood. Andrej spat the blood out on the floor.

"Fuck you asshole! Fuck you!"

The gunman was silent. "It's better than you deserve," he intoned. Andrej sat up and nursed his face with his hand.

The two sat in silence. Andrej started to get up but the gunman moved closer to him and held out the gun. "Don't fucking move, fucker. Just calm the fuck down."

"Calm down? You're the one with a fucking gun, fuck off. I got a fiance, man."

"Yeah and I used to have a son."

"What the fuck do you mean? He texted me earlier."

"Yeah, you said that. Why did he have your number? I don't recall ever texting my dry cleaning guy."

Andrej looked down. The pain was almost overwhelming. His skull throbbed from the pain and the blood streamed into his mouth. Andrej started to feel sick. His mouth watered before he threw up on the floor. The gunman moved his feet to avoid the bodily fluids.

"You're disgusting," he said shaking his head. "You're pathetic, all the guys like you are pathetic tools."

Andrej looked up at him. He dry heaved for a moment before his breath quickened.

"What did you mean by 'had a son'?"

The gunman looked up at the ceiling for a moment. He ran

his tongue over his teeth before he spoke. "I put my son in the ground today. Thanks to you."

"But, what about the—"

"The text?" the gunman interrupted. "I texted that from his phone. I wanted to make sure it was who I thought it was."

"What the fuck? He's dead?" Andrej shot back with a tone of disbelief.

"Yeah, he died, of a fucking overdose." The gunman held back tears when his voice broke. "You don't want to get that call, from a fucking cop. A fucking cop." His voice rose and he started to stand over Andrej. "A fucking cop called me at two in the goddamn morning to tell me that my son was in the hospital and they were doing everything they could to save him and I had better get down there. I ran every goddamn light and stop sign. And when I got there, I walked in and they didn't even let me see him because he was already fucking dead." His voice boomed from his throat and the words echoed off the walls. Andrej sat back, holding his jaw.

"I identified his body," the gunman said. his voice was at a normal tone again. "And today, I held my wife while she cried at his funeral and I lowered my son into the fucking ground. I had to plan his funeral. Dressed him in a suit. His buddies showed up. She's at home right now, can't calm down, won't come out of the bathroom. She hasn't eaten in four or five days."

"I'm sorry for you, but I didn't kill him," Andrej said spitting out blood again.

"Oh but you did." His voice was quiet. "You know what they found in his system? Opioids, too damn many of them, and alcohol. And that's when I found the hangars to this shop." He waved the gun in the air to punctuate his words. "So I put my son in the ground and gave him the funeral he deserved and then I decided to come find the man who killed my son." The gunman's words were measured and sure. The gunman held the gun against Andrej's skull. Andrej's blood ran cold with fear. His stomach tightened.

The gunman waved his gun around again. "You know how many of those fucking pills you sold him? Do you even know how many of those evil pills they make? Do you? Do you, fuckwad? It's on the news all the time. Millions. They make millions of those pills and pass them around like Christmas fucking candy."

"I'm sorry." Andrej started to cry. The tears flowed from his eyes. "I'm sorry your son died but I didn't kill him."

"But you sold him the goddamn pills didn't you, you worthless piece of trash."

Andrej nodded his head. "You even know how he started them?"

"No, and I don't care."

Andrej laughed at him. "You stupid fuck. He got hurt, like everyone else that needs those pills. And then he liked how he felt and he liked to party, he liked money too, he sold them shits."

"I don't give a fuck why he started them, I know he got hurt playing football."

"Then don't blame me, motherfucker," Andrej sneered. The gunman was unmoved. He pressed the cold metal barrel into Andrej's skill.

"Confess motherfucker, say it, *I sold your dead son opioids!* say it or I swear to god I will blow your brains out on this goddamn floor."

Andrej started to mumble. "I sold the pills."

"Say it, you piece of shit."

Andrej held up his hands. "I sold your son opioids, I sold him the pills, I sold him the pills." He said through the tears. "Happy? I sold him the fucking pills." He spat out the words.

"That's better."

"Don't shoot me. Please, I have parents too," Andrej pleaded.

"Do they know what you do?"

"No, no they don't. They just know I own a laundromat."

The gunman relaxed his body. "Hands behind your back." Andrej slowly lowered his hands behind his back. The gunman holstered his pistol in his jacket and pulled out some nylon rope and tied Andrej's hands securely behind his back.

"What—you going to do to me?"

"Where's your fucking phone?" Andrej nodded towards his pocket. The gunman took it out.

"Passcode."

"878787."

"Good." The gunman scrolled through his contacts until he found a contact marked, "Mama." The gunman held it in front of his face.

"This your mom?"

"Y-y—yes."

"Good, we're going to give her a little jingle and you're going to let her know what you actually do."

"No! No! No, don't do that, I can pay you, I'll cut you in, I'll do anything you want, you want my fiance? You can have her man, as many times as you want. You can fuck, she's tight, she'll do it too. I swear."

"I don't want your money, fucktard, and I don't want your girlfriend either." He pressed dial and held the phone up to Andrej's ear. Andrej started to cry. The tears streamed down his face.

"Get yourself together, you're such a worthless pussy, jesusfuckingchrist." The phone finally picked up.

"Hi Mama. Yes Mama. Listen, I don't have much time." The gunman pulled the gun out from his jacket again and placed it on his other cheek. "I have to tell you something, listen, I got into something, I-I-started selling drugs out of the shop and I don't know what to do. I know, I know, I'm sorry Mama, I'm sorry. I'll see you soon but I have to go, I'm in trouble, I just wanted you to know." The gunman ended the call. He could hear her screaming into her phone.

"Get on the ground, asshole." Andrej slid onto the floor in his own filth.

"For the murder of my son, I sentence you to death. Any last words?"

Andrej sobbed, his face stained with tears and his eyes red. He looked up at the ceiling. "I'm sorry, I didn't mean to kill anybody."

"Well you did, and now you'll pay."

The gunman held the gun to the back of his head and fired two shots. Andrej's body fell over onto the linoleum floor in a pool of blood and brains. The gunman looked at the scene for a moment. He holstered his pistol and left the laundromat. He stood outside the darkened shop. The rest of the strip mall was closed and dark. He slipped out of his clothes near his car across the parking lot and stuffed the clothes into a sack. He crossed across the parking and threw the sack into the dry cleaning shop. He removed two large canisters of gasoline from the back of his SUV and emptied them on the floor of the laundromat. He backed out of the shop, leaving the deadly liquid in his wake. He held the door open with his foot and lit a matchbook on fire. He gave it a toss and ran to the safety of his vehicle. He pulled away as fast as he could while the shop evaporated in flames. The flames danced across his mirrors as he drove away from the laundromat. He gripped the wheel of the vehicle tightly. His face bore no expression as he disappeared into the imperceptible ink of the night.

Beverly Gardens

Los Angeles is dotted with small apartment complexes, mostly built in the sixties and seventies. Although many of them have been torn down as the city grew, making the land under them more valuable than the people who lived within them, many still dot the flat landscape of southern California. Beverly Gardens had been standing in the California sun for about forty years and thanks to a lack of maintenance the stucco exterior had seen better days. The parking lot was dominated by various late model cars in various states of repair. Some of the cars had different colored body pieces and others had windows covered in plastic where glass had once been. The parking lot had been chip sealed several times and the paint on the parking spots was faded and cracked.

Apartment 301

Deb stood outside listening to her small plastic radio. "It's another great day here in LA, it's 78 degrees by the ocean, 85 in the inland empire, and 91 in the desert. It's cloudy along the ocean but we'll have clear skies today and throughout the rest of the week. Traffic is moving with usual slowing on the 5, 405 but the 101 is open. That's your traffic and weather on the 5s."

Deb stood outside and lit another cigarette. The fuzzy fabric of her sweatpants rustled in the breeze. She clasped her arms around her breasts and inhaled again. The sky was cloudy but the clouds were already starting to clear.

She flicked her cigarette into the parking lot, then started up the wooden stairs of the open staircase back to her small apartment and opened the door into the crowded space. A small traditional coffee table occupied the center of the living room. The walls were covered in a variety of posters, cloth, and some dust. Two wooden sconces hung up by thumb tacks provided cover for the plain white walls. Deb walked into the crowded kitchen. Large plastic containers sat on the counter and the sink was full of dishes. Deb put a pastry in the toaster oven before walking around the corner to knock on her daughter's door.

"Sara, it's time to get up."

"Why?"

"I got a toaster pastry heating up."

Deb elicited a groan through the door. "Besides, you need to go get your food stamps." Sara rolled over again. She pulled the thin blankets she had piled on the bed out from under her body and rolled out of bed. Her blonde hair was matted against the side of her head and she offered a big yawn.

Then she stood up and pulled on a pair of tight fitting jeans over a cheap cotton thong. She pulled a t-shirt over her head and made her way to the bathroom. She brushed out her hair and used the toilet before making her way through the cluttered apartment to the kitchen. The table was not visible under the pile of paper but an old plate with a toaster pastry sat on top with a glass of milk. Sara sta down and ate while Deb stood in the kitchen, hand on hip.

"Alright, eat fast and then I'll drop you off at the food stamp office."

"What's your shift today?"

"2-10."

"Closing again?"

"Always. They always got me closing. I think I'm the only one who knows how to close right now."

"Alright."

"Any calls for a job?"

"Not yet," she said in between bites. "I'm going to try the movie theater today."

"Are you meeting with that guy tonight?"

"Probably."

"Get $200."

"OK." she said, shoving the last of the pastry into her mouth and downing the milk. Deb walked over to the door and picked up her large, tired-looking leather purse. Sara picked up her smaller purse and they walked out to Deb's late-model van. Both women climbed in. Deb turned the key a couple times before the van finally started.

"We need to get you a car."

"I know, when I get a job I'll get a car." Deb drove through the drab neighborhood out to the main road. The sun was bright, usual for southern California. The big blue street signs reflected the light off their white letters.

Deb rolled down her window. They wound through the streets until they arrived at a squat shopping center with two levels. Sara picked her purse up off the floor of the van and opened the door.

"I'll call you when I get out of work." Sara waved at her mother. Deb drove off to work.

The heat of the day subsided by night and Deb walked out of the store towards her van, its peeling paint obvious under the yellow light. She worked to get the vehicle started and made her way through endless stop lights back to Beverly Gardens. She walked up the three flights of stairs to her apartment only to be greeted with a large official looking notice. However, she didn't need to read the contents, the title said everything she feared: *eviction*. She pulled the notice from the door. "I thought they couldn't do that anymore," she thought to herself. She opened the door and sat her purse down on the small table. She locked the door behind her and sat on the couch to look over the paperwork. The noticed stated how much rent she owed and how they had been unable to serve her or anyone over eighteen at home and therefore this notice was now required. She had sixty days to move. She put the paper on the coffee table. The surface was chipped and worn. TV remotes and some bills piled on top as well as several bottles of hand lotion, and a few dishes. She retrieved her phone from her purse and dug around through some papers. She couldn't find what she was looking for and moved her purse to the couch. She unloaded the purse until she found a worn business card for a charity that gave out money for rent help. She checked her phone but Sara had not texted her back. She put the phone away and left the business card out on the table. She opened the calculator on her phone and started to run some numbers. After some tapping she figured she could come up with $500 extra to catch up. Deb put down her phone and let the tears flow freely. She wiped her eyes and walked over to the fridge and pulled out a frozen dinner and a can of cheap beer.

She put the frozen dinner in the microwave and opened the can. She took a long swig of the beer before setting it back down. She picked up the eviction notice and read it again. The microwave rang to break the silence. She opened up the microwave and took out the food. She sat down on the couch and turned on the TV, then flipped through channels as she ate, looking at late night programs and ads before settling on a reality show. Her phone buzzed and she picked it up.

"Hey Mom, on my way home - got $300."

"OK, talk when you get here. Do you have a ride?"

"Yes, uh, sort of, a friend of the guy is taking me back."

"Alright, be safe."

Deb finished her meal. She tried to focus on the TV but the notice menaced her. She turned it over to avoid looking at it but it was there. $2474 that was due. Sixty days and they would have nowhere to go. She left the plastic remains of the dinner to sit on the table and kept working on her beer. A few moments later Sara unlocked the door and came in. She closed the door behind her and set her purse down on the coffee table. She rummaged through it as she sat down next to her mother. She pulled out some cash and handed it to her.

"Thank you," Deb said.

"Sure."

"I have bad news."

"Watsup?" Sara said, looking up from her phone.

Deb turned over the eviction notice on the coffee table. Sara looked at it before picking it up.

"So wait, we have sixty days to be out unless we pay two gs?"

"Yep."

"How'd we get so far behind?"

"Remember when I got sick?"

"Oh yeah."

Deb clasped her hands over her belly. "I'm calling these people tomorrow." She held up the business card.

"How much do you think you can get?" Sara asked.

"I don't know, I know they give out at least $500."

Sara took the card and turned it over in her hands. "OK."

"How'd the movie theater go?" Deb stood up to get another beer. She walked into the kitchen and opened the refrigerator.

"They said they'd call me but that's what they all say."

Deb shoved the door closed and walked back into the living room. "Food stamps?"

"I was approved, they said they'd mail me my card, should be here in five to ten days."

"That's good, looks like we'll have to use the food pantry too, try to figure this all out."

"OK, listen I'm going to take a shower - I feel a little gross."

"Did you eat?"

"I'm not hungry!" Sara threw over her shoulder as she entered the dingy bathroom and turned on the water.

Deb opened her can of beer and started to watch TV again. She heard Sara get out of the shower and go into her bedroom. Deb watched until the small hours of the morning before slipping into bed herself.

She woke up midday the next morning. The sun was hazy, streaming through the brown venetian blinds in her bedroom. She rolled over and checked her phone for a few minutes before finally getting out of bed. She pulled off her clothes from the night before and slipped a large t-shirt over her head. It pouched out in her middle and hung wide over her legs. She walked out of the kitchen to make coffee. She sat down on the couch and reached for the worn business card, then picked up her phone.

"Hello? Yeah, I need to talk to someone about help with my rent. I just got an eviction notice."

"OK." the lady on the other end of the line replied. "Where do you live?"

"Central LA."

"OK, when is your rent due?"

"The first."

"You said you got an eviction notice, do you have back rent due?"

"Yes."

"Alright, let me transfer you to someone who can help you better."

Deb waited listening to a piano rendition of sacred hymns.

Finally, someone picked up the phone. Deb looked around the room. Sara walked out and sat down at the table and lit a cigarette. Deb pointed outside with a scowl. Sara rolled her eyes and walked outside.

"Hello?"

"Hi - hello, this is Deb. I'm supposed to be talking to someone about help with my rent."

"Yes, I got your notes from our receptionist. Are you in immediate danger of losing your housing?":

"I just got an eviction notice."

"You should have sixty days, right?"

"Yes, but I would like to catch up so I don't lose my apartment."

"Are you on section eight?"

"No."

"Do you have a job?"

"Yes, I work in retail."

"OK great, how much back rent are you due?"

"$2400 or something like that."

"OK, there's an application, we can usually help people this week, would you be able to come down and talk with me?"

"Sure. When should I come by? I didn't catch your name."

"I'm Linda. Can you come tomorrow at ten?"

"Yes, I can do that before work."

"Great - can I get your phone number in case we need to be in touch before then?"

Deb gave her number. Linda reminded her of her appointment and looked forward to seeing her. Deb put down her phone. Sara walked back in.

"You know you're not supposed to smoke in the house."

"I know, I know - I forgot. I'm going to walk to the library."

"OK." Sara disappeared to her room for a few moments before reappearing and leaving the apartment for the walk over to the library.

Deb put on the TV for the rest of the day and played games on her phone until Sara reappeared many hours later.

"You want to come with me to the charity tomorrow?"

"Do you need me to?"

"No, I just, thought maybe you'd like to come, maybe we can get some burgers after. Before I got to work."

"Sure fine, when is it?"

"Ten."

"OK, just wake me up."

Deb checked her account to see if her paycheck had come in yet. "Not yet," she thought to herself as she looked at the balance in the app.

The next morning, she woke up Sara early and they drove down to the charity office. Deb slung her purse over her shoulder as they got out of the van and walked into the beige shopping center where the charity had set up.

"Hi, I'm here to see Linda?" Deb asked at the front desk. The space was filled with cubicles of various colors, a buzz with people talking on phones.

"Great, you can fill out this information for us while you wait? She's with another client." The pretty receptionist said, passing a clipboard with some papers attached.

Deb took the clipboard and started to carefully fill out all her details including landlord's address and phone number. Deb and Sara worked together to put down all the information and Deb wrote a note about her sickness and how they had fallen behind from her missed shifts. Once they were done, Sara returned the clipboard to the receptionist who started a file for them. After an hour of waiting Linda appeared near the desk and picked up the file.

"Deb Storm?"

Deb raised her hand and stood up. Sara followed her lead and they followed Linda back to her cubicle near the back wall of the facility.

Linda scanned the clipboard. "Have you gotten help from us before?"

"Yes, but it was a few years ago," Deb replied.

"OK, great. And you say you got sick a couple months back and fell behind?"

"That's right."

"Is this your daughter?"

"Yes."

Linda looked at Sara for a moment and smiled. "Are you working?"

"No, I'm still looking for another job. I just filled out some applications yesterday. I even called but nothing yet."

"Ok, there's some resources for that I can give you. Alright, this looks great. Is this your number?"

"Yes."

"Alright, let me take this and I'll call you with a decision here in the next couple of days, it won't take long."

Deb stood up and offered her hand. Linda shook it and Linda led them out of the building.

Deb and Sara climbed back into the van and drove off.

"Alright, let's get something to eat. Let's hope they approve us." Sara stuffed the brochures that Linda had given her on the dash of the van. The pair drove through a popular burger joint and on to Deb's workplace. The parking lot was half filled with cars and the pair ate together, listening to the radio before Deb looked at her phone and got ready to go in.

"Do you want to take the van back to the apartment?"

"I'll drive. When you do get off?"

"Ten like always."

"OK, I'll be here then. I'm not busy tonight."

"Alright, don't waste gas, can't afford it anyway."

"I won't, I'll just walk anywhere I need to go."

Deb and Sara switched seats and Deb made the long walk across the parking lot and into the large store. Sara drove the van back to the apartment. True to her word, Sara reappared at 10 pm to pick up her mother. Deb waved at her and Sara pulled up near her at the front of the store. Deb climbed in the passenger side and pulled out her phone.

"Looks like there's a voicemail." Deb held the phone to her ear. She listened carefully.

"Thank God, oh thank God."

"Was that the charity lady?" Sara asked driving out of the parking lot.

"Yes, they approved us for $400 - said they would send it directly to our apartment manager. That should help, it'll help a lot."

"Good."

"Did you get anything on jobs today?"

Sara shook her head, nothing today.

"Did you check your email?"

"No, not yet," Sara said making a left hand turn.

"You should, sometimes they email." Sara pulled the van into the parking lot and the pair walked up the stairs and into their apartment.

Apartment 401

Brenda sat in her car near the large open parking lot. A big building with old lettering spelling out "Swap meet" dominated the space. The parking lot was surrounded by trailers from various food brands. Some small signs directed people where to stand in line. A vinyl banner announced the purpose of the gathering.

"Feeding LA County: Thanksgiving Reach Out."

Brenda took a deep breath and stepped out of her car. She

gathered her purse and walked along the road until she found the back of the line. It was a mild 70 degrees. A few people had on hoodies. Women calmed children sitting in strollers as they waited to go into the area where the food was being given out. Volunteers walked around getting ready to distribute the food. Brenda stood with her arms crossed, waiting to get in. The assembled people stood there until the volunteers started to wave them in. The line started to make a circle. Each state had a different ingredient. A truck handed out bread, another truck handed out canned vegetables and other goods. The next truck handed out boxed potatoes and cake mixes. The final truck handed out a certificate to the local Ralphs for a turkey. Attached to the certificate were some other coupons for butter, milk, and eggs. Each person packed all their items in black reusable bags with the charity printed on the side. Brenda gathered all her items in her bag and stuffed the certificate into it. She looked back as she left the line. The police and the fire department had parked some equipment near the line. All the doors were open and children climbed through the trucks. Brenda saw a fireman lift a little girl into the rear cab of the ladder truck. A female firefighter gave out little pamphlets. Brenda walked past the police vehicle. Its tires came up to her shoulders and the doors stood open. She looked into the cab for a moment. The LAPD officer greeted her.

"Hi."

"Hi. Just wanted to see it," Brenda said.

"Go ahead." Brenda looked around the vehicle before starting the walk back to her car. She put the bag into the back of her car and started it. She drove down the wide boulevard to the Ralph's grocery and used the certificate to pick out a delicious looking turkey. She used the coupons and her food stamp card to buy other essentials and gathered them into her car. She started to drive home. The warehouses and shopping centers gave way to a neighborhood of small houses. The car rolled to a stop in front of Beverly Gardens. She put her car in her usual spot and carried the groceries up the stairs to number 401. She opened the door and put the groceries on the floor. She closed the door and put the groceries away. She opened a window to freshen the stale air in the apartment. She sat down on the couch and picked up the thick packet she had been sent.

"Bankruptcy 101" the first document read. She read over the paperwork again. A business card for a lawyer was stapled to the top. She picked her phone out of her purse and called the number.

"Yes, hello? My name is Brenda and I got a packet from you all previously about bankruptcy and I'd like to talk to someone about it."

"Alright," a young man replied. "Let me look at our consultation schedule."

"OK."

"We have an appointment next week after the holiday. Can you come in on Tuesday at 11:30?"

"Yes, I can do that."

"OK - great, please make sure to bring all your current bills with you and try to fill out the paperwork as best you can so we can do the best assessment of your case that we can."

"OK."

"Can I get your name and address?"

Brenda gave it to him and he tapped it out into the computer.

"Great, we'll see you next Tuesday at 11:30. Do you want a text message reminder?"

"Please, that would be helpful."

"Great, I'll set that up for you, see you then."

"Thank you." Brenda put down her phone and tapped "end call."

Brenda leaned back into the couch. She looked around the

apartment. A large entertainment center stood before her carrying a flat screen TV. The carpet was old and brown. A small round table for dining stood in one corner covered in boxes and other items. Gewgaws covered the top of the entertainment center. Glossy pictures covered the walls around her and a large Raiders flag hung behind her. She clutched a matching blanket and tucked it back into the couch.

"Happy Thanksgiving," she thought to herself.

Apartment 501

Josh sat on the toilet and let the water drain from his body. He shifted his thin frame on the large seat. He looked at the bowl. The water was clear and he flushed. He stepped into the shower and gave himself a thorough cleaning before shutting off the water and toweling himself off. He dropped the towel on the floor and looked around the empty apartment. The scene was a mess from the other guys moving out. Cardboard, papers, and empty food containers were strewn around the floor. He ignored it as he got dressed in the bedroom. He pulled on a white t-shirt and tight black jeans. He put on a red hoodie and pulled his shoulder length hair back. Josh walked back out to the living room area. He looked at the mess again and shook his head. "Fucking hustlers."

He picked up a black trash bag from a thin box that was left and piled the trash into the bag and tied the top. He gave up on further cleaning and picked up a tired black backpack from near the door. He slipped it around his shoulders and stepped out into the hallway, closing and locking the door behind him. He walked out of the apartment complex and weaved along narrow streets until he hit Sunset Boulevard.

Night enveloped the city and shops and homes had turned their lights on. Josh kept walking down the large road until he spotted the familiar dollar store where he usually met his friends. He pulled his backpack around and pulled out his phone. He scrolled through some of his messages to see if anyone wanted to meet up for sex with some generosity. He stood in the dollar store parking lot looking around for anyone he knew. He kept moving, so avoiding being a "loiterer." He rested against an old fence until he heard a familiar voice behind him.

"Hi baby!" Her voice had a sing-song ring. The tall black woman with excess makeup walked over on high heels. The streets lights made her eyeshadow glitter. She adjusted her wig with the ends of her long, purple giclee nails.

"Hi Desiree."

"Hi baby." They hugged. Josh held his cigarette over her shoulder. Her big arms enveloped his thin body.

"I have some money, you want to go have something to drink before we get these streets tonight?"

"Sure. Let's smoke first." Josh flicked his cigarette butt away as they started to walk up the street. He pulled out a small metal pipe and tucked in a few ground up leaves of cannabis. He smoked first and gave it to Desiree. Desiree took a long inhalation and handed it back. Cars drove past them, their headlights piercing the night. The pair stopped to cross Sunset to the other side.

"Let's go up to that little taco place."

Josh nodded and they walked up to the squat building. The fluorescent lights of the place were bright compared to the other closed shops in the strip mall. Desiree waved at a middle aged Asian lady walking to her car. "Hi Sandy! Thanks for coming to the show!" The woman waved back before driving off in her late model car.

"Who's that?" Josh asked.

"Just a fan. I have fans all up and down the road." The pair slid into the booth. Josh looked around the shop. An old TV, bolted to the ceiling played Spanish language television. Some fake plants sat underneath it. A pass through held sizzling food and the noise of the kitchen spilled out into the small dining area.

"Hungry, baby?"

"Uh, nah, gotta be ready for that date."

"Mhm, get your money. It's all over these streets." Desiree looked at a menu for a moment. A waitress walked over with a small order pad.

"Dos tacos, pollo, spicy." Desiree slid the menu back in its holder next to the hot sauces.

"Coke, bottle," Josh said. She nodded and disappeared into the kitchen. A moment later she returned with a bottle of imported Mexican coke for Josh. The waitress popped the metal top off the bottle in a quick motion.

"Honey, you know you never told me how'd you end up out here anyway?" Desiree said tapping her nails against the table.

Josh sipped his coke. "That's a long story."

"Everybody got long stories out here, honey."

"Yeah. Well. Don't be Mormon and a faggot."

"Oooo, you know I hate that word. There's no shame in being who you are. That's why I decided to be who I am. If the boys on my block saw me now....oh Lord."

Josh shrugged his shoulders. "It is what it is. I just have to figure out how to get a thousand before the beginning of the month."

Desiree looked outside the window and waved at someone again.

"I guess you do have fans."

"Always, baby." The waitress returned with her chicken tacos and set the chipped white plate down on the table. "Todos?" she asked. "Si, gracias darlin'!" Desiree replied with a toothy grin. She dug into the tacos and ate while Josh looked on.

"Do you have a date you're meeting or are you workin' the streets?" Desiree said in between bites.

"Both, I have a date around eleven, he already texted me, and maybe if he drops me off back down here I can get a couple more guys. It's only Friday." Desiree nodded as she bit into the tacos again.

"Sunday brunch?" she said cleaning her fingers and nails.

"Yeah, I'm cruising the apps."

Desiree swallowed the last of her taco. Josh felt his pocket vibrate and opened his phone. "That's my date."

"Alright baby, you call me if you need me. Meet up at the dollar store later?"

"Yeah."

Josh dug through his pockets for the money for his coke.

"I got it baby, don't worry."

Josh nodded and headed for the parking lot. He saw the low black car. He stuffed his phone back into his pocket. He walked over to the passenger side. The window rolled down first. Josh leaned into the window. The man was older, balding but looked fit just like in his photos. The bulge in his jeans belied his manhood.

"Josh?"

"Yeah."

"Get in."

Josh opened the black door and sat on the plush leather seat. He put his backpack between his knees.

"I know a place around the corner."

"I was thinking about taking you home tonight," he said as he pulled the car out of the parking lot and onto the boulevard. The car whizzed through a light just as it turned red.

"That costs extra."

The man pursed his lips and put his hands on top of the wheel. "That's never a problem." He slid his free hand onto

Josh's thigh.

"OK. How much?"

The car raced towards Mulholland Drive and they climbed out of Los Angeles through the traffic, the blue street signs streaking by. "How much do you need?"

"A thousand."

"Then you have to stay the night."

"Alright, let me text my friend that I'm OK, I wasn't planning on that, man."

"Yeah, yeah sure, that's fine."

Josh sent Desiree a text. "Got it big, won't be back tonight, ttyl."

Desiree texted him back almost instantly. "Get it honey, text me tomorrow baby."

Josh tucked his phone away and watched the road. The car pulled into a sleek, modern garage and pulled to a stop.

Later, the sun streaked in through the towel over the window. Josh woke up and turned over. His body ached. He stood up from the bed he had made on the floor and pulled on a tank top and sweatpants. He walked out of the bedroom and looked around the kitchen for some food. Dirty dishes, pots and pans were stacked in the sink. More food containers were piled near the refrigerator. Josh opened up the cabinets and found a box of toaster pastries and located an old yellow toaster. He put them in the top and plugged in the toaster. He pressed the button and waited. He looked around the kitchen. "Fuckin' hustlers. Fuck this." He stepped out of the apartment and onto the small balcony overlooking the parking lot. His bare feet contacted the cold cement as he lit a cigarette and waited to hear the pop of the toaster. He moved his sore body again.

"Fucker was rough," Josh thought to himself as he took another puff. He heard the pop of the toaster and went inside. He streamed cartoons while he ate his toaster pastry. In between pastries he loaded his small metal pipe and smoked more cannabis. When the high hit his blood stream his body quit aching. He stretched out. He looked around the room and started to feel anxious about the mess. He stood up and stretched his arms over his head, then grabbed another trash bag and started to pick up all the trash in the living room. Soon all the trash was picked up leaving only the dirty, formerly cream colored carpet. Josh stood up with the bag and leaned against a poster of a generic muscle man in a speedo. Josh looked at the poster for a moment. He looked around the other bare walls.

"Guess it's mine now," he thought. He put the bag by the door and moved to the kitchen. He was taking out all the dishes when he heard a knock at the door. He rubbed his eyes, shut off the water and walked over. He looked the peep hole.

"I got your money," he spoke loud enough to get through the door.

"Hey, um, I'm not with the building, I'm from downstairs, your neighbor, can you open up?" Sara said.

Josh opened up the door and stood in the frame. Sara wore a faded t-shirt and tight fitting jeans. "Hey did you seen the notice on your door?"

"What notice?" Sara pointed at an official looking piece of paper on the door. Josh pulled the paper off the door and looked it over.

"Sorry, I have trouble reading, fuck my adhd and dyslexia."

"It's OK. Basically, they're tearing the down the building and we all have like three months to be out or whatever."

"The fuck?" Josh said finally getting clarity about what he was reading. "Yeah, ninety days here in bold."

"I guess, yeah, anyway, do you know anything about this?"

"Nah, I don't know shit. Fuck," he said.

Sara pulled on her hair. "OK, um alright then. My Mom is

talking about trying to have a meeting and seeing what we can do. I'll let you know so you can trade a shift or something?"

"Uh sure, yeah, whatever, I'll try to be there."

"OK cool." Sara waved at him as she started for the metal stairs. Josh closed the door and carefully read over the paper again. He looked up at the wall. His mind went blank for a moment. He put the paper down and smoked another bowl of cannabis. "Fuck this shit." He said out loud. He stood up and finished his original project. All the dishes were washed and sitting in the drying rack. He went over to his backpack and thumbed through the money again. He laid out all his money on the floor. He counted it out carefully. One thousand, three hundred and forty dollars.

"Stay or go," he said out loud to himself. He gathered the money up and put it back in his backpack.

Can't Afford to Stay, Can't Afford to Go.

The tenants started to gather in the small room. Sara spread out all the old metal chairs she could find. Brenda sat in one chair and looked around the room. Deb pulled out some packages of cookies and put them on a heavy wooden table on the back wall of the room.

A neatly dressed young man in a hoodie and a t-shirt came in. His long red hair was pulled up on top of his head.

"I'm looking for Deb?" She raised her hand. "Hi, I'm Nate with LA Tenant Advocates."

"Thanks for coming. Everyone is still coming in."

"OK. Great."" Nate smiled and stood near the food. He greeted different people as they came in. People piled the snacks on the little dollar store paper plates and sat down around the room. When most of the chairs were filled he stood at the front of the room and held up his hands.

"Hey Deb, is it OK if we start?"

She nodded her head. "Alright, I want to introduce myself. I'm Nate I'm with the LA Tenant Advocates Alliance. Deb, your neighbor, asked me here to tonight to talk about your building possibly being torn down for new development and what advocacy we might be able to provide to help out with that. Why don't we start with some introductions maybe and any questions you might have. Oh does anyone here speak Spanish? Do I need to repeat it?" One woman held up her hand and he repeated his speech in perfect Spanish. Nate asked if she had a translator with her. She pointed at her daughter and he smiled. "Alright, let's get those introductions underway." He clasped his hands and looked at Deb. She started the introductions and people went around the room until everyone introduced themselves. People spoke quietly and stated their name and sometimes what they did. Josh sat in the back of the room and looked around.

"I have the first question," Deb said when the introductions were over. "Can they do this? Is it legal? Do they have to provide something?"

"That's a great question. We're going to get talking about a tenant association in a bit, but let's attack the question. According to the Los Angeles Rent Stabilization Tenant Relocation Assistance Ordinance they have to provide assistance if the building was built after 1978. However, I did some pre-research for this meeting and that's where I have some bad news. This building was built in 1976, just before the deadline, so I don't think you guys qualify. I'm surprised that no one has taken advantage of this before now honestly, given how fast LA has grown since '76."

"And it survived Northridge too," Brenda added.

"Yeah, exactly." Nate looked around the room for the next question between the quiet munching of snacks. A few kids sat in the corner and played amongst themselves.

A Hispanic woman asked a question in Spanish. Nate nodded his head. "So what she asked was what was going to happen to everyone if they couldn't find other housing in the next ninety days. That's an area where we can help. We can be a resource for those who are looking for affordable housing options around the area."

Brenda raised her hand. "I know you mentioned a tenant association, but, some of us might end up homeless. I'm in the middle of having to file for bankruptcy due to some medical bills and that means it's going to be hard to get another apartment. I just can't believe they can do this, some of us have been here ten years."

"Right, so sorry for your struggle. Our goal is to help tenants work with their landlords to keep housing fair and equitable and give tenants a voice. The sad reality is that with all the new growth, I'm going to meetings like this all over the city. Lots of older landlords are getting attractive offers from developers. This is becoming a pretty common story."

Sara raised her hand. "Can we fight it or stop it?"

Nate held his hands behind his back and looked at the floor a moment before nodding his head and beginning his answer. "It's possible but that means hiring a lawyer and bringing a case to court. Because of the age of the building, the compensation law doesn't apply and the owner has a right to sell and demolish the building so I don't really know how that would go, I'm not a lawyer, but that is an option that could be explored, however, it's not cheap either, even with our lawyers."

"So basically there's nothing we can do and we all have to move," Josh said from the back of the room.

"I would say options are limited and I think it would be a good idea to work with everyone on housing options." Nate said. "However, if you guys want to have a meeting with your landlord and talk about options, I can help facilitate that for sure."

Brenda shook her head. "Don't they get these are people's homes? Moving isn't cheap."

Nate nodded his head, "I get it. I've been in a building that went through this too. There are other organizations that can help with moving expenses or even low cost truck options and things like that. I can connect you to those." Nate waited a moment. "Other questions for me?"

No one raised their hand. "Alright, I'll be around for a little bit if you want to talk to me privately. I know speaking in front of a group of your neighbors can be intimidating. I brought cards and resources to help with this transition, please make sure to take them. I want to help as much as I can. I'll be at the back." Nate walked to the back of the room. The group clapped for a moment. The group started talking to each other. The Hispanic woman walked up to Nate to talk to him. Josh slipped out the back of the room and nodded his head at Nate as he made his way out of the small room towards his apartment. Brenda stood up shaking her head. Deb motioned to Sara to follow her and the group slowly filtered out of the room. Deb and Sara put the chairs away. Nate waved at Deb. "I'm going to head out."

"Thanks for coming and helping us, most people don't want really help anyone like us."

"It's not a problem, it's what we do. I see people took a lot of the resources which is going to help. Please don't be afraid to give me a call."

"Thanks, uh, we will."

Judgement Day
Judgement Day was like any other southern Californian day. The air had a tinge of smog. The radio DJs blasted the latest hits around vapid callers and the ever-present sun shone down on Beverly Gardens. The early spring day was pleasant but

slightly cool. Most Californians would don a hoodie to combat the chilly 70 degrees.

Deb and Sara woke up that morning. Most of what they needed was already packed in the van. Deb rolled off the bed and rubbed her eyes. She let out a long yawn before checking the time.

"Got time before that truck gets here," she thought to herself. She pulled on clothes and walked out to the mostly empty apartment. She knocked on Sara's door. "Breakfast, do you want any?"

"You woke me up!"

"You need to be up anyway, that truck's going to be here in an hour. I'm going to McDonalds."

"Bring me back something."

"I'll get you a number two."

"Ok, cool, whatevs."

Deb walked downstairs and towards her van. She passed Brenda in the parking lot. Brenda looked at her own car and shuffled some items around. Brenda waved at Deb.

"Did you find a place?"

Brenda shook her head. "No, I didn't. My bankruptcy is in progress and no one would take my application, bad credit. So it looks like I'll be living in my car for awhile. I found out about a safe parking lot where I can park and I guess figure things out."

Deb touched her arm. "You have any kids?"

"A daughter, she's living with her boyfriend up in Chico, no room for me there."

Deb pulled out her keys. "Sara and I are lucky, we found a place, just barely. I think we're about it. Everyone else left awhile ago."

"Yeah, Marilyn in 504 ended up in a nursing home, her kids made her."

"Did you hear where Maria ended up?" Deb asked.

"I didn't but they moved out last week," Brenda said closing the back of her car. "Probably family or something. I still can't believe this is happening. I just can't."

Deb held out her arms for a hug. Brenda embraced her for a moment. "Good luck, I'm getting some breakfast before the truck comes."

"You too, with your new place." Deb waved at her, keys in hand, as she squeezed into her packed van. The two women drove off out of the driveway and onto the streets. Deb returned a few minutes later with breakfast. Sara and Deb ate together in the kitchen. Then they took the keys off their keychains. The truck arrived and they helped take out the bed and other small furniture. The truck was loaded and Sara dashed upstairs to leave the keys on the counter. She closed the door behind and slid into the van with Deb and they started towards their new place.

Josh woke up to afternoon sun and took one last shower. He left the water fall onto his shoulders and stream down his body. He washed his hair before stepping out of the shower. He wrapped a towel around his waist. He looked around the apartment for a moment to see if the other guys had already gone. Their backpacks were not there. "Good," he thought to himself. "Makes it easier." Josh pulled on some clothes and made sure that everything he needed was in his backpack. He looked at the poster of the underwear model again. He stared into the model's blank eyes for a moment.

He moved out to the small balcony and lit a cigarette. He held the cigarette with his teeth as he packed a bowl for the day. He finished his cigarette and flicked the butt out to the parking lot. He sparked up the bowl, edging it carefully and letting the high sink into his bones. He checked the place one more time. He grabbed his laptop and some personal items out of the bathroom and stuffed them into his heavy backpack. He leaned against the door and stared at the bare apartment. He plucked out his phone and texted Desiree. He looked out the sliding door towards the squat buildings of his neighborhood and beyond. He wanted to wait for the sun to fall but the paper had been clear. 5 p.m. was the deadline. He checked his phone. He had an hour. Wait or go? Josh decided to start walking. He slung his backpack over his shoulders and tossed the keys onto the kitchen counter. He opened the door and passed over the threshold. He let the door close behind him and started out to the streets passing the wooden "Beverly Gardens" sign for the last time.

The Beverly Gardens chip-sealed parking lot was empty. No cars stood with hoods open, waiting for their owners to work on them. The grass on the east side, where the children usually played, was quiet. There was no smells of cooking food, or couples having a fight. There was no sound of people coming up and down the stairwells to and from work. No music thumped the walls. No one talked in the breezeways.

A few days later, a fence went up around the property. The Beverly Gardens sign came down first. A banner was hung to advertise the demolition company and a large bin sat in the parking lot as the men began the process of tearing the building down. Another sign was soon added announcing the new development. The march of progress had laid down its next step at the property formerly known as Beverly Gardens.

Windswept Wastes

I drifted here. I drifted there. I grew up in New Jersey but I never stayed anywhere too long after my wife left me while I was in Vietnam. I went over there, two tours, 25th infantry, April 10, 1965 to June 14, 1966 and then I went right back from September 11, 1966 to October 5, 1967. I was at war and she was bedding down a guy who was 4F, bone spurs or some shit like that. I meanwhile was 1A, prime fighting stock. We were only married to avoid the draft anyway, but then they started drafting married guys and I was in it. I didn't mind. Saw some horrible shit over there though.

I drifted into Denver in early 1968. I had left California because shit was getting weird. I was tired of dodging hippies, war protestors, and the lot. I was working at a car factory but that place was fucked up. Everyone drank on the job and no one cared if they actually did their job. I'm not like that. I like to do a good job. The job was nice though. I was in paint but then they moved me over to door seals. So then I was gluing the rubber door seals on all the doors. I liked being in the paint shop better, though. It was fun. You just got a gun with paint and every car body that came in you just sprayed the whole thing down with whatever color was supposed to go on it. I miss the paint shop but I don't miss the fuckwads that worked there. Those folks had issues. That's why I left. That was a GM plant too. Good cars mostly, you'd be surprised how many times they had to fix cars that were new. Wrong body pieces and all sorts of stuff. It was weird.

Anyway, I tried out Wyoming for awhile. I liked the wide open spaces but Wyoming didn't fit me. So I decided to try out Denver. Took me a bit to get down there on account of the snow but I finally rolled into town about February. I tried my best not to get my car stuck in the snow. I got me a Pontiac GTO, I love that car. It just flies, just flies. Anyway, I finally rolled into Denver. I started to look around for a job. I was sleeping in this motel off Colfax. There were some great bars along there. I hung out there for awhile but I needed a job pretty soon. Motels ain't cheap you know and I gotta eat. I like to eat. That's when I met David. David was a cool guy. He was out of California like me and he knew a place that always needed guys who could work. I met David for coffee the next morning. He told me where the diner was on a street called Colfax. I found him sitting in the back of the place against a painted brick wall. The place looked real modern, you know with those shaped lights like how they have them. We ordered food and coffee and David pulled out a city map.

"So just take this road here, out here and turn right. There's nothing out there so just keep going along this here until you see the big white sign that says, "Front Range Chemical Facility."

"How long is it?" I wanted to know what kind of drive I was signing up for.

"It's about an hour, but worth it, they start you out at $7 and you can get up to $9. Healthcare too."

"That's damn good money, what do they do out there."

"That's sort of a secret. If you get hired, they'll tell you. I will tell you that it's real exciting."

"Secret? Come on man, it can't be that important."

"Nah." David leaned in towards me. "They make you sign stuff. You have to promise not to tell anyone what you actually do. Most folks don't even ask anymore. When you say you work out at Front Range Chemical, they know not to ask any more questions."

I leaned back and took a sip of coffee. "Alright, alright. I'll take a cruise out there."

"You should."

I finished my coffee out of the thick cup. I gave the waitress a solid up and down. She was young, cute, and kept the coffee cup filled. I appreciate that in a woman.

"Yeah, so just cruise on out there, it's pretty country too. There's a bar out there called Rocky Flats. Most everyone that works out at Front Range Chemical stop off there for a drink after work because it's a drive to get home."

We finished our breakfast and I looked out towards the busy street outside.

"Those women working?"

"Yeah, but if you need company I can give you some numbers."

"Yeah, maybe, I'll call you later."

"Alright man, call me after you head out there."

"Cool, alright."

I put a few bucks on the table and walked out to my car. I pulled out a city map and traced my route. I turned onto Colfax and started the long drive out to this place. I passed under the Valley Highway and started my drive. The signs for Colfax Ave gave way to signs for US 40. I passed neighborhoods first and some turn offs for different buildings. The strip malls reminded me of Cali a little bit. The city dropped away too and revealed the rocky desert surface. The mountains grew as I kept driving towards them. Finally I reached my turn off. I made the right turn and laid down the gas along the windy road. I passed a defunct mining operation and I wove my way through the hills. I finally passed the bar he mentioned. I knew I must be on the right route and kept driving. I saw the sign but I was going too fast to make the turn and I stopped short. I looked around the deserted road and decided to just back up to make the turn. I pulled up to the guard shack and came to a stop. I cranked down the window. The guard walked out and spit on the ground.

"Badge?"

"Don't got one. I heard you guys were hiring and I'm looking for a job."

"Aight, go here, take a left and go to building 4, that's HR, if there's any openings then they'll help you out with that. What's your name?"

"Michael. Everyone calls me Mike."

"Alright Mike, let me make you a visitor's badge." The guard disappeared and scrawled my name on a visitor's badge with a small logo on it.

"Gladys Chemical, that the company here?"

"Yeah, that's us, building 4, see you in a bit."

"OK." I cranked the window back up and guided my car over to the left. A small "4" showed on a building and I pulled up near it. I stepped out of the car and tucked in my t-shirt. I swiped my hair back again and walked up to the glass and metal door. The name of the place was painted on and beneath that it said, "Human Resources."

I walked in and looked around for a moment until I saw a desk with a girl sitting at it. The Gladys Chemical logo was plastered on the wall behind it.

"Hi, I heard you guys were hiring."

She clasped her hands. "We are, um, what do you do?"

"This and that, I've worked in an auto factory doing paint, worked in machine in the past. I weld. If it can be welded I can weld it together."

"Alright, let me look through our current positions. You

can fill out this application while I do that." She handed me a clipboard with a thin, plastic ballpoint pen attached.

I walked over to the metal and cloth chairs and sat down. I filled out the application and watched her look at some papers and walk around the building. She re-appeared and waited for me to finish filling out the application. I signed the bottom and walked back to the counter.

"Here you go."

"Thanks. If you wait a few moments I'll look over this and talk to my supervisor. We have a few positions open. Are you a veteran?"

"Yes, yes I am." She smiled back at me.

I finished the application and I left it back at the desk. She took the clipboard from me and looked it over. She disappeared into another office for several minutes.

"Mr. Lindsey will see you now."

I stood up and walked into the office. The man sat behind a large wooden desk. The carpet was thicker than the floor out in the office and I looked down at it for a moment before extending my hand.

"Mr. Lindsey is it?"

"That's right, and it looks like you're Michael?"

"Michael Campbell, that's right."

"Alright." He shook my hand over the desk. The secretary closed the door behind her with a smile.

"It looks like you've got plenty of work experience. And it looks like you'd be a good fit. Why do you want to work here?"

"Well, I'm just new to the area and met a guy who said you guys always need people so I figured I'd try it out."

"I see, well, we do need a competent welder, are you very accurate?"

"Accurate enough for cars, and you have to be accurate, quality control don't tolerate bad welds, especially on frames."

"Good, good, we run from 8 am to 6 pm, is that a problem?"

"No sir."

"Overtime?"

"Always welcome."

"Are you married?"

"No sir, but I might have to ask your secretary out."

He smiled at that remark. "Very good then, alright, you can start tomorrow in the welding shop. Come back to this office tomorrow morning at 8 and I'll introduce you to the welding foreman."

"Thank you sir." I stood up and extended my hand again. He gave it a firm shake and I let myself out of the office. I stopped at the desk.

"You wouldn't know of any closer motels would you? I drove out from Denver. Seems a bit far."

The secretary smiled. "There's a phonebook over by that telephone, if you'd like to look before you leave."

"I was hoping for a personal recommendation."

"Most of our workers live in Arvada, it's the nearest town. You'll find something there."

"Alright. You want to go out for a drink tonight after I get a little closer?" I leaned over the desk and rested my arms on it while trying to look her in the eyes. I could see that under that suit, she had a nice body. A body I'd like to see more of.

"I don't get off until 5. But I'm seeing someone right now."

I backed away from the desk. "Alright, well, I had to ask, see you tomorrow." I walked out of the building and I could feel her watching me go. I walked back out to my car. I heard a horn sound and a few men walk out with their lunch pails. I drove out of the gate and turned in my badge and started my journey back to Denver. I spent the rest of the day looking for a new motel. I found one near that Arvada place she talked about. The town was cute. There was a little hamburger stand and a small downtown area. There was a couple bars off the main street and some train tracks ran right through town. Denver stood off at a distance with thin roads leading towards the city. I looked around the town as I drove through it and I thought it would do. I found a little motel and checked in. Since I hadn't had any luck with that little secretary I decided to drive on over to a little bar next to the Army Navy surplus shop and have a beer before getting ready for my first day of work at whatever this chemical place did. I picked up a hamburger from the little shop and enjoyed my beer.

The drive the next morning was much easier and shorter. I cruised right out to the plant and arrived just about 8. The man at the gate gave me another visitor's badge and I walked into the HR office, lunch box in hand, ready to see what the welding shop was like.

Mr. Lindsey walked out to the front room and waved at me. "Michael, there you are. You actually showed up, some guys don't even come back." That secretary was already standing there with a camera. He motioned over to his secretary.

"We need your picture for your official badge. We'll have it for you at the end of the day."

"Alright." I smoothed my hair down and stood up straight. She took my picture in front of a white wall behind her desk and smiled at me. The flash popped and I shook off my stiff posture.

"Let's walk over to the welding building and we'll get you started. Good to have you aboard." I followed him deeper into the complex, over to building 17, and he opened the small door and showed me a massive welding shop. Men were covered in thick aprons and had their welding helmets on working on various small pieces of metal. Mr. Lindsey tapped a man on the shoulder.

"Halsey, Halsey, I got that new guy I told you about."

The man lifted his hood and looked over his shoulder. "Yeah?" He put down his tools.

"Halsey, I'm the foreman here," he said. "You know gas tungsten?"

"I'm familiar, we used gas metal on cars but I've used gas tungsten before mostly on aluminum."

"Alright, did he sign the paperwork yet?"

"No, you should take him to sign it and give him the safety briefing."

"Powell, wrap this up. I gotta go do paperwork."

Halsey waved me towards him. Mr. Lindsey shook my hand "Thanks, welcome, Halsey's the foreman in the welding shop, so if you have any problems just let him know."

Halsey led me into his small office. The place was crowded with papers and books. His desk was covered in files. I sat down in one of the chairs.

"Alright, let's look here, let's see, new employees." He dug through some files and found a stapled packet of paperwork and opened a file in my name. He put a sticker on the top and wrote my name.

"I used to have a secretary to do this shit."

"What happened to her?"

"Quit, that happens a lot around here. No one has been hired to replace her."

"What about that girl over at HR?"

"Don't get me started, they should have had you do this before they took you over here."

He put a thick stack of paper in front of me.

"They tell you what we do here?"

"No, everyone acts like it's some big secret or something."

It is," Halsey said flatly. "I need you to sign this agreement that you will keep your work here to yourself and to keep any information you learn about this facility and what we do here to yourself. If you're caught talking about it, you can get federal time for it and no one wants federal time."

I sat back for a minute. "What do you guys do here?"

"Sign that and I'll tell you."

I looked over the paper and it stated about what he said but in more legal language.

"OK." I signed the bottom of the paper and gave it back to him.

"Thanks." He signed the other side. "You know about shop safety?"

I nodded my head. "Yeah, GM harped on that pretty hard, so did the union."

"Good, wear your protective equipment at all times when you're on the floor, you see someone doing something stupid, you tell me. Our work needs to be accurate and I don't mean good enough, I mean it has to be perfect otherwise it gets sawed off and you start over."

I shrugged my shoulders. "OK, fine, not a problem."

"Yeah, no bullshit, when we fuck up people die, right here too."

"Jesus Christ, what are we making here?"

Halsey leaned forward. "We make the cores that go in tactical nuclear weapons."

I didn't know what to say at first. I hadn't really thought about how they made the bomb, just that we did make them. "Don't they do that in some secret place?"

Halsey laughed and revealed some missing teeth in his bottom row. "Yeah, and we're part of that secret place."

Halsey stood up and opened the office door. "You'll start with me, I'll show you the basics of what goes where and how to put it together and then I'll set you off on your own tomorrow."

I followed him out to his work bench and he pulled off a project. He pointed over at a rack of safety clothes and pulled on a helmet and apron and joined him at his bench. "Like this, along these lines here." I followed his pattern and he wasn't joking about accurate. I hadn't seen that nice a weld on a Cadillac.

Lunch rolled around and the horn sounded. The whole shop put down their tools and started out of the place. Halsey had me setup at a bench working on some pieces. I followed everyone out and walked over to my car to get my lunch. I saw that most of the guys sat at some picnic benches around the back of the building. I sat down with my lunch and picked out my food and looked around the otherwise desolate area. Halsey sat down and introduced me around.

"This is the new guy, Mike Campbell. That's Harvard, we call him that because he worked there once, that's Prinz, Mexican but we like him. Then there's Fredman, Phillips, Moore, and Saxon, in our little group."

I nodded and shook hands all around.

"You want to stop by the bar on the way home?" Harvard asked.

"I was planning on it anyway, so sure." We ate our sandwiches and I stood up to stretch. The horn sounded and we all trooped back into work. The rest of the afternoon, I carefully welded on the bench and had my work checked by the foreman. He seemed pleased but I was ready for the shift to end. Harvard touched my shoulder as I started to walk out.

"You know where the bar is?"

"Yeah, it's that little place on the road back to town?"

"Yeah, that's the place. Can't miss it." I kept walking to the car and looked forward to a nice cold beer.

I started the car up and drove out of the parking lot. I drove down the long stretch of road towards the car. The parking lot was already pretty full by the time I pulled in. I parked out back and walked into the crowded bar. I found the bar and ordered a beer. She handed me a yellow can marked "Coors." I had never heard of it before but it was alright. I took a look around the bar. I found the guys from my shop and joined them at a table. Saxon took a big swig of his beer and lit another cigarette.

"You hear that they are planning doubles next week?"

"Good money," Prinz said with a smile.

"Yeah, true, but long days pisses off my wife," Saxon replied.

"My wife likes money too much," Prinz said with a laugh.

I paid partial attention to the conversation. I hated doubles but money is money. I was looking for anyone single in the bar. I was especially looking for that pretty secretary I saw on my first day. I didn't see her. I guess she really was seeing someone. You can't fault a guy for trying, right?

The guys from my shop filtered out to go home to their wives. I stayed a while longer. I played pool and shot some darts until the bar started to empty out. I decided to make my way to my new apartment myself. I slid into the seat of my car and set out on the dark road to Arvada.

The work was alright. Each guy had a pile of parts to weld and after a few days it became pretty routine. Halsey checked my work often but soon he saw that I was competent. I could tell some of the other guys weren't experienced. They were making some simple mistakes. Halsey spent more time walking around making sure our group did our job than he spent welding his own parts.

I avoided all that during working hours. I just tried to keep my head down and weld quality parts that wouldn't get sent back by quality control. I noticed, at the end of my first month that many of the parts got sent back and soon, my bench was half and half. Half new projects and half ones that needed to be fixed for various problems.

I kept the same routine. Work all day, hang out at the bar after work for a few drinks and go home. But after a few months I started to notice that there were some new faces around the shop. It was good work and it paid alright. Harvard explained it all to me one night at the bar.

I finished my beer and got us two more. I was starting to like Coors.

"You were talking about why they hire so many new guys?"

"Yeah," Harvard said, taking his beer from me.

"Basically, Dow can't keep people. The job is in the middle of nowhere, everyone has to commute forty five minutes to an hour just to get here and then there's the whole matter of just working with people who don't know what the fuck they're doing."

"You think the pay would keep people."

"Nah, our group is OK because Halsey is a standup guy, but not all the facilities are like that."

"You work elsewhere in the plant?"

"Yeah, I bounced around when I first got hired until I settled in at the welding shop. I just don't think they don't get how to make this stuff, everyone is doing stuff and the pressure is on to make more and more of it even though what we do isn't fast. Things happen, guys get hurt and they quit or they just can't put up with the bullshit and quit. Either way, they quit."

I took a long swig from my beer. "So why do you stay?"

"Halsey, that and the money. My wife likes the check so she puts up with rest of it."

"You mentioned that."

Harvard rested his elbows on the table and stared off into space. I interrupted his gaze.

"Lose you there?"

"Yeah, thinking about a Dodgers game."

"Fan?"

"Since they were in Brooklyn."

"Yeah, they were the team at the GM plant I was at."

"Now that's a good job."

"If you're at a decent plant."

Harvard nodded his head and drank some more beer. "I hear that. That why you left?"

"Yeah, that place was insane, people drinking on the job, tons of problems, ran out of parts all the time and people just did dumb shit. Wrong front ends on certain cars, no weather stripping, it was fucked up."

Harvard drained his beer. "I think I'm going to go home and fuck the wife."

I held my beer up. "Get it."

Harvard smirked as he threw down some cash. "We got three kids for a reason."

I finished my beer as he walked out of the bar and looked around. The other guys were long gone. Just a few people stood around. Even one of the pool tables was open. I walked over and started to shoot some pool. No one came to bet me. I played two breaks before I decided to make the drive back to town. Harvard was right. The drive was long. Longer in the dark.

I managed to book some major overtime and by midsummer my checks were getting pretty fat. I moved out of the motel and into a real apartment. I even bought some furniture: the lady at the store helped me pick it out. I got a TV and started to hang around the little downtown on weekends. Denver was pretty close by. I could get in the car and cruise into the city and see what was happening. The city had seen better days. Lots of brick buildings, most of them empty and lots of empty streets, especially once you got away from the state capitol. The gold dome was pretty neat. I stared at it for awhile trying to figure out how to get up there and scrape some of it off and head for Mexico.

The ten hour days were wearing everyone out but August set

in and I saw a poster on the way into the shop announcing a Safety Ball. The days without an accident had gotten up there, we'd gone a couple months without one and somebody decided it was time to celebrate that. Halsey made a point of talking about it.

"Mike! You coming to the safety ball?" Halsey sat down with us at lunch outside on the benches. The wind whipped around us but it didn't stop us from eating.

"I guess. Don't have a suit though."

"Yeah, you should get one. You're one of the reasons our safety days are so high, we got decent workers like you and it's nice to eat free company food and drink free company beer for all that overtime you've been putting in." He bit into his sandwich. "Bring your wives, get dressed up, it's a good time."

The guys nodded. I thought about the prospect of shopping. This is where having a wife is nice. She gets to do this stuff for you. We finished work. I decided to skip the bar and find a Sears or JCPenney to buy a suit before the big safety ball. I stopped by the office for a phone book and looked up some local stores. I found a mall that looked promising and decided that was my best bet.

I set the GTO on the road again and started for the big mall. I drove through the suburbs of the city until I found the Villa Italia mall. The outside was white with tall white columns. I pulled into the big parking lot outside the JCPenney store and started in for the men's section. The store was not terribly busy. The big lights reflected off the white walls. It looked bright and friendly. I found the men's section and started to look at the suits on the plastic models.

"Can I help you?" I looked up and down the pretty sales assistant.

"Yeah, I have a work event. Need a suit for it. It's one of those things."

"Of course." She turned away from me. Her hair fell around her shoulders in effortless waves. It bounced when she moved.

"This is our best seller. It's simple and easy to wear."

"How much?"

"This is $45 for the jacket and slacks. The shirt is $5 and the tie is $1.50. For two dollars more, you can get a French cuff style shirt and we can select some cufflinks. The suit is made from dacron, it's a very nice fabric." She held out the suit towards me. I reached out and touched it.

"Alright, I guess I should try it on."

"Of course. Do you know your size?"

"Not really."

"Let's measure you then!" She smiled and took out her tape measure. She wrapped that little tape around my chest, along my shoulders and around my neck. She measured my legs as well. She selected a suit from the rack and showed me to one of the men's fitting rooms.

I tried the suit on and it looked about right. I didn't look like a welding man. I looked like a smart office guy. I carefully removed the clothes.

"I'll take it, no cuffs though, just the regular shirt. I guess I need shoes too."

She smiled as she took out her pad to write it up. "Let's get you rung up and I'll walk you over to men's shoes. Are you sure I can't talk you into some French cuffs? They are in this season." She started towards the counter. I leaned against the counter and looked at the display of jewelry in the glass case. Pairs of cufflinks were perched in boxes.

"Well, some of those cuff links look cool."

"Here, let me show you one of the shirts." She put the suit on the rack and walked to the shirt section for a moment. She returned a moment later with the shirt and took out a smart pair of silver cufflinks. "See? That goes on your wrist. If your work has these regularly you can rewear them often or if you're going out with your wife."

"I'm not married but you've talked me into. I'll go with the French cuffs."

"You'll look really nice with them. Cash or charge today?"

"I'm new to town, it's cash today."

"Do you want a credit application anyway?"

"No ma'am, I don't really use credit. I keep things cash."

"Alright, with the suit, French cuff shirt, tie, and cufflinks your total today is $58.13."

I counted out the bills from my wallet. She took my money and gave me the change. I pocketed the change and she packed up my new clothes.

"Do you want to leave this here while you shop for shoes and socks?"

"That'd be convenient."

"Of course, not a problem. I'll put it aside, just come pick it up when you're ready to leave. Name?"

"Mike."

"Alright. Let's walk you over to men's shoes." I followed her over to the shoe department. She introduced me to the man, who fitted me with a pair of black patent leather shoes. She stayed on my mind while I got the shoes and socks to go with them. I paid for the shoes and hurried back to menswear to pick up my suit. She was still there.

"Ready to go?" she asked when she saw me walking over.

"Yeah."

"I'll get your suit." She disappeared into the back and came back with my suit neatly packed up and a bag with my shirt, tie, and cufflinks.

"Here you are Mike. It was a pleasure serving you tonight."

I took the clothes from her. "When do you get off here?"

"Eight."

"Got plans tonight?" I asked.

"Maybe. I put my number on your ticket."

"Alright then. I'll give you a call." I smiled at her.

I walked out of the store and back to my car. I laid the bag and the suit out in the trunk of the car. I shut it and made my way back to Arvada.

She did come for that drink and she stayed the night after in my new place. I woke up the next morning to go to work and she woke up with me. I kissed her long and hard as I slid into the GTO to head out to the plant.

Halsey reminded us of the safety ball that Saturday at lunch.

"Yeah, I got my suit last night, met a real pretty girl too."

"The single life..." Harvard let his voice drift off.

I turned towards him. "You miss it?"

"Yeah, you know, sometimes."

"You ever, you know, step out."

"Nah." Harvard took a long drink of his water. "Not worth it."

Halsey smiled. "Good man. You're lucky."

Harvard shrugged his shoulders. "Grass ain't always greener."

"That don't stop you from taking that Playboy subscription."

"Don't hurt to look!" Harvard said, stretching his shoulders back.

The horn sounded and we all trooped back in to work. I kept welding my parts and fixing the bad ones. I noticed that Halsey was bringing in some new faces again. I tapped Prinz on the shoulder.

"New guys again?"

"Yeah, you taking overtime tonight?"

"Yeah, gotta pay for that suit."

Prinz nodded, put down his hood and kept welding. I worked late that night and eventually got out of the shop and drove back to Arvada. I called my pretty sales girl.

"I caught you." I leaned against the chair and stubbed out a cigarette.

"You did."

"The other night was great."

"You were good too, I liked it."

"Listen, my job has a safety ball on Saturday night, you know that, that's why I bought that suit."

"Yeah?"

"I thought I'd invite you to it. Dress pretty though."

"Sure, pick me up?"

"Alright, I'll do that."

"OK. You better take down my address."

I scrambled around for a pen and paper. I found a pen and an envelope.

"Alright, pick you up at six."

"Alright."

"Good night, Nancy."

"Good night Mike."

I replaced the black receiver on the cradle and leaned back in my chair. I felt excited now.

They had us working overtime for the rest of the week so I didn't get out of work on Friday until almost eight. I drove home and flopped into bed. I woke up on Saturday morning with plenty of body aches from a week of ten and twelve hour shifts. I got moving so I could get my hair cut. I took a shower and washed off the grime. I cashed my check and got my hair cut in the little downtown area. I walked around for a little bit and watched a couple trains go by before heading back to get dressed.

I put on the suit and I looked real clean and fresh. I combed my hair to the side. I don't think I'd looked as fresh and clean as when I left boot.

I drove to Nancy's apartment and picked her up. She looked

real pretty in a long dress and a little purse. Her hair was done up and she sat down in the car just like a lady. I closed the door and we drove into Denver to the big hotel for this party.

I pulled the car up to the entrance of the hotel. The facade looked modern with an interesting concrete screen in front of the drive. I opted to skip the valet and parked it myself after dropping Nancy off at the door. We followed the signs into the ballroom. Gladys Chemical signs hung around with a big sign that read, "90 days of Safety!" on the back wall. Balloons and bunting in the company colors made the place feel festive. Nancy hung on my arm.

"You didn't say you worked at Front Range Chemical."

"Uh, yeah, I do. I weld stuff."

"Oh, I didn't know they had welders at a place that makes scrubbing bubbles!"

"Oh sure, of course."

"I love that stuff!"

"Drink?"

"Let's get one!" Nancy said starting for the bar.

Nancy floated across the floor to the bar and I followed along. She ordered a highball and I got a simple whiskey. Music from the band filled the air and added to the festive mood. We were about half way through our drinks when I spotted Harvard and Prinz. I held up my glass to wave them over.

Harvard and Prinz walked over, wives in tow.

"Halsey here yet?" Prinz asked.

"I haven't seen him. We just got here, got a drink."

Harvard and Prinz introduced their wives. Nancy shook their hands. I was impressed. She was good at this. They got their drinks and soon a waiter passed by with some food on a big tray. Nancy removed two of the little snacks, one for me and one for her. We had just bitten into the food when I saw Halsey walk in with his wife. I waved him over.

"Did you guys find the welding shop table?"

"No," I said, swallowing.

"Yeah, each department gets a table or tables, come on." Halsey looked around the room. Each table had a small sign I hadn't noticed before. He pointed. "There it is, Welding." We walked over to the table and Nancy sat down as I pushed her chair in. She set her pretty hand bag on the table.

The party was soon in full swing. I took Nancy out to the dance floor and we danced two dances before the formal dinner started and the bosses started into some boring speeches I tried not to pay attention to. The food was alright and the booze was free. Nancy was having a good time and I liked that. I liked everything about her. I liked how she talked and how she walked. I liked how she dressed and I liked how she was, as a person I mean. I hadn't met someone like her before. She wasn't like my ex-wife. She was warm and outgoing.

The dinner came to a close around nine thirty, I think. I could tell it was late because Halsey was starting to yawn. The music started to die down and I walked out to get the car. I whistled as I crossed the big parking lot to find my car. I drove around to the front of the hotel where Nancy stood with the others. I opened the car for her and we started driving out of downtown Denver. I slung the car around the tight curves of Speer Boulevard.

"Do you want to stay the night or go home?" I asked her as I shifted into third.

"I have to be up tomorrow. There's a sale on shirts in casual wear," she said flicking her cigarette ash out the window.

"I can always stay with you."

"I think I'd like that."

I drove back to her apartment and parked outside. We walked up the metal stairs to her second floor apartment. She unlocked the door. I kissed her as she bent down to work the key. She giggled.

"Alright, alright," she said as the door gave way. Her apartment was decorated simply. She let her bag fall on a chair and she dashed into the bathroom. I took off my jacket and loosed my tie. She reappeared in the living room in her slip and nothing else. I took out my cufflinks and put them in my pocket for safe keeping.

I like how she curled up next to me, nice and safe. I smoked a cigarette and let the smoke driftup towards the ceiling. I stubbed it out and finally fell asleep, Nancy lying up against my flesh, warming my side.

When I woke up, Nancy was already gone but there was a note.

"Had to work, please lock behind you, key is under the mat. Had a great time, call me. XO, Nancy."

I threw on my clothes and grabbed my jacket. I locked the door shut tight and drove back to my place. I had worked most Saturdays for the past couple months so I was looking forward to a day of actual relaxing and possibly a nap.

I bought beer and some cigarettes and waited to call Nancy in the evening. By Monday I was ready to get back to my welding at work. Two days off in a row was nice and the party was a nice way to take a break from the speed we'd been working at for awhile. However, when I arrived at the Welding Shop, Halsey waved me over to his office.

"Morning. Problem?"

"Nah, listen, they need some guys in building 72 so I actually wanted to talk to you about changing jobs."

"What's the job?"

"Close the door."

I closed the office door. "It's the plutonium fabrication building. that's where the real magic happens, that's where they actually make the cores that go in our parts."

"Sounds dangerous."

"It's $1.50 per hour more than here in welding and seeing how you're actually competent, they are desperate for decent workers over there."

I wasn't sure how I felt about working with the real stuff. But the money was attractive. $1.50 wasn't bad either.

"Ain't that the stuff that makes it, you know, explode, the bomb I mean."

"It is, that's why they have to have guys who know what the hell they're doing."

"Yeah, OK, I'll do it."

"Great, I'll let the plant manager know."

I walked out to the shop and started in on some flawed parts. By the next day Halsey was walking me over to building 72. The place was not well lit at all. I noticed right away that the building was filled with these long glass enclosures with holes in the side.

"This is Jimmy, he'll be your new foreman. It was nice working with you, Mike."

"See you, Halsey, say hi to the guys for me."

Halsey held up a hand to acknowledge me.

Jimmy held out his hand towards me. "Mike, is it?"

"Yeah."

"Halsey says you're a good worker, says he hates to lose you."

"Yeah, Always work hard."

Jimmy took out a little square piece of plastic and stuck it to my collar. "You'll need one of these, we wear them at all times."

"What is it?"

"It's a dosimeter badge, it tells us if any radiation has infiltrated the air at unsafe levels. If this turns yellow, it means you've been exposed and we need to shut down the facility and do a cleanup."

"Uh, OK."

"It's all apart of the training you'll be going through. We even have a glove box for you to practice in."

"Is that what those big things are called?" I said pointing at the long boxes.

"Yes, also there's no smoking on the floor, we smoke outside." Jimmy led me through the building past the men with their arms stuck inside those glove boxes. They stood on stools as they worked. He led me into a room where he put on a training film. They had filmed the entire process of what they did and what each job was. He gave me a pad to take notes in. I took sparse notes on the process. It was complicated, more complicated than welding. By the time I was done watching his movies it was about lunch time. I decided to eat lunch with the welding shop instead of these new guys I hadn't met yet. I wouldn't meet my first real co-worker for about another week. Jimmy was right. They had a training glove box. It was hard to work with. The glovers were thick and rubbery. I sat for hours getting practice at holding things and pouring liquids and working with fake sand meant to work like plutonium. There was a regulation for everything. How everything happened had to be precise. I didn't realize that the stuff would burn at room temperature either. Everything had to be done a certain way. I thought GM was anal retentive about how to do things, this was even more complicated than building a car.

It took me about two weeks before I completed all the training steps required for my first day on the line with the real material. By my second week I had gotten handy with those blue rubbery gloves. I had perfected pulling my hands out without pulling the glove out of the box which could cause a radiation release. I started to wonder if the extra $1.50 was worth the trouble and the constant threat of turning the whole place into Nagasaki.

After the two weeks of training, I started my first day on the line. Jimmy led me over to my new station at the glove boxes.

My chair was already set up and the gloves were at the ready. He tapped my new coworker on the shoulder. He removed his hands from the glove box.

"Frank, meet Mike, he's going to be working next to you."

Frank nodded at me.

"Hi. They train you?"

"I think so. Just did two weeks on the practice box."

"Good, that's more than the last guy."

Jimmy smiled. "Show him the ropes, they liked him over in welding."

Frank nodded his head and put his arms back in the glove box. "This is the part of the process where we pour the plutonium into the molds. See the molds there in the box?"

I put my arms into the box and looked through the clear top for the stack of molds.

"Yeah, I got them here."

"Alright, we usually just pass things to each other within the box, once it goes in it can't come out, so if you need something just ask."

I started working. Working within the box was like working with a very dangerous chemistry set. I carefully poured my first mold and then added the additive to make it set in the mold. I found a pile of rags nearby and wiped off the excess to form a perfect button. The material was about the size of half an orange but that small amount could lay waste to the whole place.

It was sweaty work, the gloves didn't breathe and your hands started to feel like those jungles in Nam after forty five minutes. It was an assembly line so everyone took their break together, lunch too. I didn't know anybody yet so my first day I just ate on my own. After a couple days, Frank got brave and decided to sit down for lunch.

"No one's still talking to you, huh?" he said, opening his lunch pail.

"Yeah, not a friendly bunch," I replied.

"That's because no one stays around long, guys move on, it's hot work and stressful."

"Yeah, what's up with the heat?"

"The A/C doesn't work too well, never has really, they need to do something about it. Would make it easier since your hands are in those gloves, might as well be wearing big thick nylons."

"Yeah."

"Smoke?"

I took out my own pack and pulled one out.

"I always try to smoke two at lunch, that way I can last until break."

"Good idea."

We smoked in silence until the horn sounded and we all marched back in and took our places at the glove boxes.

After a few days I started to get real handy with those gloves and I kept pouring the mixture into those forms real regular. I got good at passing things around the glove boxes and some of my co-workers on the line even started talking to me. It was hot work. I hadn't sweat that much since Vietnam but my check was getting fatter and that was good. Making the stuff was a slow methodical process and overtime was a regular thing you could get if you wanted it. I picked up Frank's job, too: if he couldn't stay I could switch between our boxes and do both jobs pretty well. Cleanup was the toughest part of the day. Everything used that couldn't be used again, like those rags, had to be passed to the end of the box and put in a special part of the box where it could be sealed off from the rest of the line and then removed for waste storage. From what I could tell, they just stored it out back in big barrels. It didn't seem real safe considering what we were dealing with but the bosses knew best anyway so I just focused on working on my buttons. I was happy to work at it until one day when everything just went wrong.

It was on a Thursday. I had plans with Nancy that weekend. I was liking her company and I thought that maybe it was time to get serious, with a girl like her, you don't let those ones get away. I was starting to see a future with her. I wanted that future and she made me want to settle down from my drifting ways. I was liking Colorado life. All that fresh air and sunshine. It was like California without the Hare Krishnas.

I was working late and Frank had stayed so we were working together. I had wiped off another button and sent it on for packaging at the next station down the glove box. It was late summer and it was hot. The A/C wasn't keeping up and the building was metal to start with. The last thing I remember was taking out my hand to wipe off my face so I could finish the button I was working on when I saw one of the guys jump off his chair and away from his station. I never heard an alarm but someone shouted fire. I looked to see where the fire was and then I realized that the fire was inside the glove boxes. I could see smoke smoke start to fill the long boxes. I pulled my hands out of the glove box and ran towards the fire. The glove boxes were full of smoke. One of the guys was already on the floor, grabbing his face. Two guys drug him away from the line. Jimmy screamed "Get the extinguishers!" We mustered at the fire fighting station. We helped each other into our fire suits and we returned to the glove boxes with our extinguishers. We turned them on the flames sprouting from inside the line of boxes and tried to put out the fire but the fire raged on.

Water hoses were added to the fight and we used everything we had to stop the flames. The room was becoming contaminated with nuclear material. Different guys fell from the heat and exhaustion. I knew from training that it would be on everything, now that the glove boxes had been broken. I tried not to think about that part. We worked on the fire in shifts.

We couldn't go outside to get air and take a break. We just took turns holding the hoses. I had never seen fire burn green before. I had never felt that heat before. I imagine that's what being in a nuclear blast would be like if you could live to tell the story. At some point the ceiling started to give way and Jimmy directed the water to the ceiling.

"The building has to fucking stay sealed!" he shouted at us. After what seemed like hours, the fire finally started to die down and after some more cleanup effort, the fire was out. Everything was either waterlogged or black. Our suits had dosimeter badges like we always wore and they were bright yellow. We had all gotten a nasty dose of radiation. The cleanup for us was intense.

By this time, some government men had come by to help with the aftermath and they put us in these showers and scrubbed us with big brushes, ass naked. They wore special suits like we had. It's never fun getting scrubbed by two men in space suits. I thought showering with guys in the army was bad enough, somehow this was worse. They tested each of us for radiation before they let us leave. We were given some thin clothes to wear because our clothes were ruined. I was lucky, my jeans passed so I only had to take a t-shirt. Some of the other guys phoned home to get clothes. They scrubbed my boots and they passed too so I was able to leave with some dignity.

When I was finally allowed to leave, I walked out into the dark and windy Colorado night. The parking lot lights moved with the wind. The parking lot was empty, just a few cars remained. I gimp-walked over to the GTO and slid into the seat. Couldn't start it at first. I was hot, tired, and I hurt all over. Everyone else had left. They probably made everyone leave considering we about blew the whole place up. I started for the bar. I needed a goddamn drink. I called Nancy from the bar and told her about the accident without giving her too many details. She met me at the bar near my apartment after she got off from the store. I was on my fifth beer by that time.

"Oh baby, are you alright?" she said clinging to my shoulders.

"Yeah, I'm alright, I'm alright. it was just a fire."

"Who knew making cleaning products could be so dangerous?" she said sitting down next to me at the bar.

"Industrial accidents happen. Not often, but they happen."

"I'm just glad you're OK." She rubbed my arm again and then ordered a drink of her own. I smoked my last cigarette from the pack.

"Thanks for coming. It means a lot to me."

"Of course, I don't want anything happening to you."

"I don't want anything happening to me either."

Nancy smiled, in that sweet way I liked. "Let's finish this drink and then let's go back to your place and relax."

"Alright. I'd like that."

"Good."

Nancy and I got back to my place. I was a bit sloshed. I needed to clear my head and Nancy helped me with that. I didn't have to go to work the next day and I just stayed home. I watched some TV and stared at the wall for a bit. For the first time since Nam, I was scared. Somehow, that fire was worse than the gooks and the jungles. Nancy called me after she got off work.

"How are you feeling tonight?"

"Good, I guess."

"You OK?"

"I think I'm gonna quit."

"Yeah?"

"Don't think I can go through that again."

"That must have been some fire, you seem really shaken by it."

"Yeah, I haven't even drank today."

"Do you want me to bring some beer over?"

"Yeah. That'd be nice."

Nancy showed up with beer, true to her word. She dressed real pretty for work and I got to enjoy the view. I appreciated it. I opened one right away and drank about half of the bottle.

"You don't seem OK."

"I don't know."

Nancy put her hand on my shoulder and I reached up for it. I pulled her into me and we cuddled in silence on the couch. I finished the beer and broke the embrace to get another.

"Was it a bad fire? The news said it was a bad fire."

"Yeah, the whole place is toast. Wait, it was in the news?"

Nancy shook her head. "It was. You guys don't make scrubbing bubbles, do you?"

"No, we sure as hell don't."

"They said it could have poisoned everyone." Nancy's voice edged with concern.

"Yeah, it could have, but we stopped it," I said downing more beer.

"I'm glad you stopped it."

Nancy stayed over again. I got drunk trying to get those images out of my head. I never thought I'd see something worse than the jungles but that fire was worse. I'd take a rice paddy again over that shit any day.

On Monday I drove out to work and walked into the office and said I was quitting and picked up my final cheque. That Mr. Lindsey didn't even try to stop me. He just handed me my cheque and shook my hand. I left my badge on the counter and drove out of that place about as fast as I could. I didn't want to see Front Range Chemical ever again.

I stayed in the area after that. Nancy and I eventually got married. She gave me a reason to stop drifting and settle down. We got a little house in Arvada and raised two good kids. I did end up going out to the plant again but it was different. In the 70s, they started protesting out there. The fire had gotten the word out about what they actually did there. All those hippies I left behind in California started protesting out there and I decided to join them. They blocked railroad tracks by laying on them. They even surrounded the place by holding each others' hands around the place. They were strange but good people. They really had beliefs about things. I soon realized that maybe I didn't understand them. They weren't all the same and not the same as the kids who spit on us coming back from Nam. We didn't need war. I had seen war. It's grisly. Your buddies get their legs and arms blown off. You just hope that you get to go back safe. I was one of the lucky ones. I didn't leave any body parts in Nam. That place was always in the news until they finally closed it in '91 after nearly restarting the civil war out there. Turns out I was right: they never did fix the A/C and no one ever told me that plutonium burns at room temperatures. All those rags we used were just fires waiting to happen. It wasn't anyone's fault, no one had a fucking clue how to make that stuff.

I still think about that fire. I think about all that radiation we all got. But then I have a lot of time to think, these days. My days are spent in doctor's offices and chemotherapy appointments anyway. I heard there's a lawsuit happening but they can't find anyone to sue. The government is fucking around with any kind of help or settlement for everyone who worked there. Plant's gone too, all cleaned up now. Just a nature preserve. They hauled all the waste off to Nevada or New Mexico or something like that. I still can't believe they just buried it out back. We all got a nasty dose every day we worked there. I'll never forget that fire.

Sanctuary

Kevin stood on one pedal of his bike and let it roll to a stop. He pulled up the hood of his hoodie and rolled his bike towards the garage. He tapped in the code and the door rose up. He dropped his bike in the garage and started into the house and upstairs to his room. He closed the door behind him and slipped off his backpack. His bedroom floor was littered with clothes, a few bottles, and books. His phone buzzed. He ran his hand through his blond hair and stripped off his shirt off his, youthful toned body. He tapped the screen.

"Reeeeee." Kevin smiled. Darren always did that to say hello.

"Coming over?" the next text read.

"Yea, just changing and shower, I'm ripe."

"Good - I don't need that shit in my car. I found a cool spot to party, you in?"

"Yea, maybe, girls there?"

"Supposed to be, we can check it out."

"And they want more guys."

"It's not that kind of place, anyone cool is welcome, thought you might want to get some, bro."

"Yeah, cool, uh, how long?"

"Text when you're out of the shower."

Kevin climbed into the shower and washed quickly, then dried himself off. He rubbed the towel over his mop of hair and slid into some loose clothes and pulled a fitted cap over his hair so it stuck out around the edges.

He heard his mom pull her big SUV into the garage. He looked at the pile of unfinished college applications. "Fuck," he thought to himself.

"Kevin? Kevin!" He heard her shout. He kept quiet. He tip-toed around the room. He sprayed a fresh cologne and texted Darren.

"Alright, gimme 10."

Kevin scrolled through social profiles while he waited.

"Here."

"K, gotta get around my mom."

"Fence."

"Yeah, have to get downstairs first."

Kevin listened to see where his mom was. Hearing nothing, he quietly moved through the house and made his way to the large sliding door. He walked out of the back patio and hopped the fence into the street. He jogged down the streets until he found Darren's car. He pulled open the passenger door and slid into the passenger seat.

"Hey, man."

"Let's get out of here." Darren put his foot to the floor and the late model BMW chirped its tyres as he pulled away from the curb and into the open street. They drove along the quiet suburban streets, past manicured lawns and large SUVs parked in driveways. The spring evening was pleasant but Darren kept the dark-tinted windows on the car shut with the air on.

"Do you want to smoke now or when we get there?"

"Let's just do it there, if it's as cool as you say."

"Yeah, sure. I think it's around here." Darren drove slowly until he saw the pathway leading down into the concrete gully. He pulled to a stop and looked around. He pulled onto a sidestreet and parked the car at the edge of the road, far enough away from the stop sign and fire hydrant so as not to get a ticket. Then he rolled his long body out of the car and onto the street. Kevin hoisted himself onto the curb and looked around.

"Over there." Darren pointed towards the path they had passed. Darren looked over the edge and started down the path. Kevin followed him and they passed through an entrance made of scrap metal and old plastic cans.

The entrance took the boys under a bridge to some open space. Large concrete culverts stood in neat lines, never installed. The area was sixteen feet or so below the quiet road, where no one would notice. Kevin looked around. Christmas lights hung in between the concrete ovals and he could smell cooking food. Kevin and Darren passed a group of girls sharing a cigarette. The smell of a grill changed to weed as they walked.

"Welcome to the sanctuary!" Kevin's head snapped towards the voice.

"Hi, I'm Dolph." He held out his hand towards Kevin. Darren held out his hand. "I'm Darren." A black lab stood behind Dolph's legs, tail wagging back and forth.

"Oh yeah, I think I was texting you. You picking up at all? Don't be afraid of him, he's scared of new people."

Kevin raised his hand, "Yeah."

"Forty an eighth, good quality stuff, I have full nugs of it too. Nice and dry, no bullshit."

Kevin reached into his pocket and pulled out two crisp twenty dollar bills. He held them up. Dolph took them from him and pocketed the money. He reached under the grill for a metal box and set it on the side of the grill. He opened the box and paused to turn over some of the meat he was grilling. Once the meat was turned over he opened the box and pulled out a cigarette for himself and plucked out a scale and a bag. He weighed out the green buds and packaged them neatly in the sandwich bag.

"There you are, my man."

"Thanks."

Darren pulled out a small piece of glass from his pocket. "Let's smoke." Darren, Kevin and Dolph took turns smoking the fruity cannabis and Dolph started pulling meat off the grill. He set it on an old plate. He turned off the gas and walked the plate, piled high with meat, over to another culvert where some mismatched chairs and small tables stood on a large rug. The scene was almost romantic. The Christmas lights hung across the top of the concrete structure and the inside had been festooned with thin tapestries screen-printed with mandalas.

"You guys hungry?"

Darren and Kevin nodded. "I can eat," Kevin replied. Dolph leaned out the open end of the culvert. "Food, motherfuckers!" he shouted.

A few other young people sauntered over and sat down. Cigarettes were put out outside the space or in a nearby ashtray. Some of the girls sat on the floor of the space and others took up the remaining chairs.

"Amanda and Justin not coming?" Dolph asked looking around.

"I think they're fucking again," one of the thin girls said with disgust. Kevin let his gaze drift over to her.

"Hi, hello, I'm Jenna." She waved at Kevin.

"Hi. Kevin."

"Hi Kevin." Jenna took a paper plate from Dolph. A bratwurst in a bun stood on the plate. She reached for a bag of chips. Kevin picked it up and handed it to her. She poured out some chips. The food was passed around the group until everyone had some of what they wanted. The little room was quiet while everyone ate. Jenna looked out the end of the culvert after finishing her food.

"Justin! Amanda! Food!"

The tardy couple walked over and sat down on the floor. Dolph gave them some food.

"Hi, that's Kevin and his friend - what was your name?"

"Darren?"

"Yeah, that's them, they're new."

"Hi, I'm Amanda, this is Justin." Justin nodded as he took a big bite. Darren loaded another bowl and passed it around for an after-dinner dessert.

"Beer?" Justin asked.

Dolph pointed to a cooler that stood outside the little room. Justin rooted around in it for a beer. The cans and ice clashed against each other. "Anyone else?"

A few hands went up, including Darren's. "He'll have one too." Darren pointed at Kevin. Justin passed around the beers.

"They way we smoke, you'll need to re-up before you guys leave." Dolph said with a smile as he inhaled. He released the opaque smoke a few seconds later. It hung in the air before finally dissipating.

"Dolph, music," Jenna said. "I need music."

Dolph stood up and adjusted his pants. He left the little room and started walking over to another Culvert. Vaporwave music started to flow through the air. The tin sounds smoothed out with muddy beats permeated the whole space. Dolph returned looking at his phone.

"Looks like more folks are showing up soon. Time to get this party started."

"I'm doing shots. Amanda, let's go get the tequila. Kevin, why don't you come with us to Amanda's car?"

"OK." Amanda put down her plate and stood up. The two girls left and Kevin followed them. The group started to spread out. Smokers stood outside having an after dinner puff.

Kevin followed Amanda and Jenna. Amanda wore a simple

dress with flat shoes. She looked feminine and yet simple. Jenna in contrast wore tight fitting jeans and a long t-shirt with Converse. The trio arrived at a small SUV. Amanda unlocked the doors and Jenna took out a bag. She slung it over her shoulder and smiled. "Let's drink." The trio walked back towards the path that led them back to the group. They saw a group of five people descend the pathway and through the entrance. They walked back into the empty dining culvert and sat down. Jenna looked around for some shot glasses. She found some plastic ones and set them on a small table. "Here, you drink." Jenna said, pouring out three shots.

"Uh, sure."

"What, you've never had tequila before?" Amanda asked.

"No, I don't think so, just like fireball and jaeger."

"Then your night is about to get a whole lot better," Jenna said as she picked up her shot glass.

"I wish we had salt."

"Don't be stupid, Amanda," Jenna said downing the shot. Amanda drank her shot, shrugging her shoulders. Kevin picked up his own shot glass and let the liquid burn down his throat. He coughed at the end.

"There you go. There's a lot more where that came from. Where's Ben?"

"I'm going to find Justin." Amanda stood up and walked out.

"She's so obsessed with that kid. It's sad. You play anything?" Jenna crossed her legs and looked at Kevin.

"Football in the fall, track in spring."

"Nice. You seen the whole place yet?"

"Nah, just here and over there."

"Come on, I'll show you around."

Jenna stood up and took Kevin's hand. He followed her out of the little room and into the open area. "So that's the music room, sometimes people will go in there to play music and that's where the sound system starts. Then, over there are the bedrooms. People sometimes stay the night here and if you want to have sex or whatever. That's the smoke room, there's bongs in there or whatever, hookah too, and back here is the theater." Jenna led him behind the bedrooms towards an open area where a large TV stood. Two guys were sitting in front of it on camp chairs playing a video game.

"Slash gaming too, I guess. I guess someone got their xbox hooked up."

"We should check out that smoke room. I just picked up." Kevin offered.

"I thought you'd never ask."

The pair walked over to the big culvert and ducked inside the curtain. Dolph sat in a plastic chair lighting a long bong. His feet rested on another thick, imitation Persian rug with multiple stains.

"Hey Dolph, Kevin wants a pipe."

Dolph finished his hit and held his breath. He finally exhaled a long tail of smoke. "Here you go buddy," he said in between light coughs.

Kevin took the pipe from him and packed in his own weed and lit up the bowl. The water trembled as he inhaled and the tube filled with smoke and then disappeared into his lungs.

"Fuck," he choked out. He passed it to Jenna. Jenna leaned out the end of the culvert. "Amanda! Smoke! Amanda!" Amanda appeared moments later as Jenna lit her own hit and inhaled a smaller hit than Kevin. Amanda kept the cannabis burning and inhaled for herself.

Dolph leaned against the back of the chair and rested it against the grey wall. "This is the life. I fuckin' love the burbs, you can get away with everything."

"This your thing, right?" Kevin asked.

"Yeah, I found the spot, got power to it, everyone contributed something to it, though. Like the rugs and shit came from a guy whose Mom was getting rid of them so he offered to quote-unquote haul them off for her and I got 'em instead!"

"That's cool. How'd you decide this was a party spot?"

"Why not? The city isn't using it and these were just standing here doing nothing and it's fuckin' private as fuck, you can't see it from the road until you're on top of it and there was already a little path to get down here."

"Cool, too bad you can't like live down here."

Dolph laughed and picked up the heavy glass again. "Who says I don't?"

Kevin nodded his head. "That's cool. I hate living out here, everything is the same."

"Where do you go to school?" Dolph choked out the question as he exhaled again.

"Keller prep," Kevin responded.

"Ooo, private. Nice," Jenna said. "We both go to Yellow Valley."

"Private school, man, I did that when I was your age." Dolph said looking up at the ceiling. He rubbed his legs for a moment before letting his chair fall forward and looking at Kevin.

"You want to know the real reason I created the Sanctuary?"

"The what?" Kevin asked, leaning forward.

"That's what this place is, didn't you see it on the sign?" Amanda said before she used her lighter to take another hit.

"I guess I missed it."

"Listen, man," Dolph stared at Kevin. His eyes were low but Kevin locked into his gaze. Kevin felt his body get light and didn't break the connection between them.

"The suburbs are full of all sorts of rumors. In the 90s, it was people that jumped fences at night and ran through yards. Another rumor that got passed around were drug dealers hiding stashes in the yards of unsuspecting mid-level account executives who might come across it on their way to warming up their Toyota Camry."

"No shit?"

"It's all bullshit, though. People are just afraid that their nice quiet little lives might get interrupted by actual life. The suburbs have a quality that masks collective humanity. As long as the yard stays neat, the leaves get cleaned up and snow gets shoveled, no one really bothers to look beneath the quality results of repeated trips to Home Depot. This makes hiding things like drug addiction, child abuse, and alcoholism pretty easy. As long as you can perform the motions of suburban life, everyone agrees not to ask too many questions. All the houses and fences are far apart enough to give just enough privacy that you can drunkenly yell at your wife and as long as you aren't too loud, you can get away with it. The suburbs are so bland that some people, especially teenagers, like you, ave to do something to reclaim their humanity."

Kevin instinctively let his hand brush across his chest and up his neck and through his hair. "I get it, I get it."

"That's why I started the Sanctuary. It's a place for the beige siding to end and for actual life to begin. You can bring your booze, you can bring your drugs, you can fuck. Just be cool. Just be cool. I don't care what you do. You just have to live and get along with people. Folks bring food. Sometimes I barbecue like my dad, just like tonight. It's all love, it's peace, it's finding yourself. That's why it's a Sanctuary."

"Fuck yeah! I love it when you talk like that, Dolph!" Jenna said, raising her fists in the air. "Fuck these houses and fuck these places, this is real, this is happening."

"Anybody seen my buddy?" Kevin said looking around. "Haven't seen him in like, awhile."

"Not that long, man, you've just lost track of time. It's all good."

"He'll turn up. We watch out for each other here," Jenna said rubbing her hand on Kevin's leg. Kevin lowered himself down to the floor to sit next to her. Dolph lit another bowl and kept smoking. The music started to fade and he stood up in a swift motion. He finished taking his hit and started over to the music room to keep the tunes going.

Kevin stared off into space for a moment. Darren pulled back the curtain and entered the smoking room.

"Hey."

Kevin didn't reply for a long moment. "Hi."

"Someone's high as fuck, I need to catch up." Jenna pointed at the heavy piece of glass. Darren filled the bowl and took three long inhalations before offering the glass to others. Amanda and Jenna took hits of their own before Jenna broke out the tequila again and took a long swig from the bottle.

"What are you guys doing this summer?" Darren asked.

"Where's Justin?" Amanda said, dodging his question.

"Hanging out here probably," Jenna said.

Kevin looked over at Darren. "Working out, probably, hanging out, new Madden out."

"Dude, I already know what you're doing!" Darren said smiling. "I was asking the girls."

"Sorry, spaced out."

"Come back to us," Jenna said leaning onto him. Kevin opened his arm and she rested her head on his chest. She pulled his phone out of his pocket. "Unlock please." She held up the phone to his face for a moment. "Thanks." She put her number into his phone and stuffed it back into his pocket.

"You're comfy. I could get used to this."

Darren kept smoking and Amanda stood up. "I'm going to go look for Justin." Amanda disappeared out of the smoke room. Darren cached the bowl and left Jenna and Kevin alone in the smoking room.

Kevin let his head hang down on onto her head.

"Ugh, Amanda is after Justin again. Typical. He's like air for her. She can't live without him."

"Yeah, that's always annoying."

"For sure."

Silence enveloped the room for a bit and the lights twinkled. Jenna rubbed his jeans. She brushed his crotch with her hand.

"You want to check out one of the bedrooms? They're cool."

"Sure," Kevin replied making his first attempt at standing. Jenna stood up easily and helped him onto his feet. She took him by the hand. Darren was standing with another group of girls and gave Kevin a thumbs-up as they passed. Kevin gave him a quick smile. Jenna led him over to one of the culverts, placed a little bit away from the rest. A thick piece of cloth hung over the entrance. Jenna pulled it back and guided Kevin inside. A big rug covered the bottom of the structure. Pillows and an old mattress stood on top. Blankets and more Christmas lights finished the space. Jenna turned around and put her hands on Kevin's chest.

"This should come off." Kevin lifted his shirt off his chest. He embraced Jenna and his hands ran up to her back until he found her bra clasp. He fumbled around with it for a few seconds.

"Let me help you there."

"I suck at those."

"Yeah, me too honestly." In one quick motion she loosed the underwire bra and lifted it and her shirt off, revealing her breasts. Kevin walked forward a few steps, pushing her towards the bed. He kissed her and let his mouth wander over her body. She inhaled sharply. The pair lay down on the bed and continued exploring their bodies. Jenna didn't hold back with her moans. The pair climaxed together and Jenna let the weight of Kevin's body rest on her. The moment was broken when

Kevin heard Darren shouting outside.

"Cops! Fucking Cops! Dude! Run! Fucking run!"

Kevin popped up and pulled on his clothes. Jenna grabbed her clothes and slipped them on. She didn't bother with her bra and stuffed it in her bag with the tequila. Kevin and Jenna ran out of the room and into the open. Darren pointed at the cops rummaging through the Sanctuary.

"I gotta find Amanda," Jenna said.

"Dude, we gotta go, we can't get arrested."

Jenna let go of Kevin's hand. "Text me and add me and shit." Kevin leaned down and gave her a kiss. "Yeah, yeah, your number's in my phone, cool."

"Go, I'm gonna find Amanda."

Darren and Kevin sprinted off. They circled around the back of the culverts and crouched down. The cops passed by them with flash lights and when a cop was a few feet away from them they burst out running. They ran away from the culverts and over a drainage area. A small stream ran along the bottom. The grassy sections on either side allowed them to run. One of the cops started to chase them.

"Stop! Freeze! Police!" Darren and Kevin didn't stop. They kept running. Kevin looked back for a moment to see the cop lose his footing and fall into the stream. Kevin ran like a track star. His arms were purposeful and his feet consistent. Darren used his long legs to gain distance from the scene. The drainage area gave way to some baseball fields and the pair climbed out of the concrete drainage area and up onto the street. The lights of the cop cars illuminated the night. The strobes seemed to light up the night sky.

"How the fuck are we gonna get my car?" Darren said in between heavy breaths. He balanced to catch his breath.

Kevin walked around, his chest heaving. "Wait them out?"

"Fuck, dude. Where?"

Kevin looked around for some place to hide but his attention was brought back to the camp when a small explosion ricocheted through the air. A scream could be heard after the fireball burst into the air and extinguished into black smoke. More sirens could be heard as fire trucks began to pull up to the scene.

"Fuck. What was that?"

Kevin jogged back a moment. "The propane tank probably."

"Aww, fuck, man, fuck, who called the fucking cops?"

"Maybe someone in those houses." Kevin pointed to a stand of houses near the camp on the other side of the street near where Darren's car was parked.

"Yeah maybe, either way, we need to get out of here before the cops come down here."

Kevin and Darren started walking away from the camp. Kevin pulled out his phone and texted Jenna. "Are you alright?" He waited for a reply. The pair kept walking until they found a big gas station and convenience store. They walked into the bright store. A friendly Indian shop keeper greeted them. "Hello!" Kevin and Darren nodded. The pair bought water, energy drinks and some snacks, paid for them, and walked out to the back of the store and sat down against the wall.

"We have to get back to my car, dude."

"Yeah, it was like thirty minutes to get there. We could get an Uber or something."

Darren didn't respond for a moment. "Yeah, I don't want to get into all that with my parents."

Kevin checked his phone again to see if Jenna had replied. The message was marked delivered but unread. Kevin let his head rest against the brick.

"Hope she got out," Kevin said.

"You get some?" Darren asked opening his energy drink.

"Yeah, we just finished when the cops showed up."

"Nice, man." The pair high-fived. Darren took a long swig of his energy drink.

"Yeah, it was good."

"That puts you up to what? Lucky number ten?"

Kevin thought for a moment, "Yeah, like ten I think, maybe eleven."

"Losing count already?" Darren snarked.

"Fuck you."

"Fuck you, too" Darren replied, drinking more of his energy drink. The pair sat in silence and let the world pass them by for several minutes. Cars came and went in front of the gas station. Delivery trucks broke the quiet of the night.

Kevin stood up. "Wanna go get your car?"

Darren looked around. "Yeah, we gotta look out for cops, though."

"Sure, sure."

"Let's walk, see if we can find our way back."

"It's along that creek, so if we find the creek we can find your car."

The boys started to walk back to the Sanctuary and Darren's car. The lights of the gas station faded into the background and soon they were in the dark embrace of the night, dotted with light from the street lights on the corners of the quiet suburbs. Unlike the city, the suburbs were quiet. There was no honking of cars or yelling of drunk people like a busy city – no, the suburbs were quiet. Families slept in their box-store derived beds. Sheets from other box stores covered them. Their kitchens were filled with food from wholesale clubs and practical but useful cars stood in the garage or occasionally the drive way. The lawns were neatly manicured. Kevin and Darren heard the gentle swish of sprinkler systems watering those prized lawns.

Kevin and Darren didn't want to draw attention to themselves but it was unusual for anyone to be walking around at night. They stood out as the only humans on foot in the middle of the night in a place that was designed with big wide roads for driving, not walking. People walking is what they came to the suburbs to escape. Why experience the world in your face when you could experience it from the safety of a metal and glass bubble?

Darren and Kevin both stretched as the high and alcohol wore off. Their minds and bodies returned to the mundane plane of existence. After forty five minutes of solid walking Kevin sighted Darren's car. Darren crouched down. Kevin followed his lead.

"See any cops around here?"

Kevin peered into the night. "No. I don't think so."

"Let's walk slow, look at all the cars, you see cops, we run."

"Yeah."

Darren and Kevin walked along the road next to the creek. They saw the culverts come into view. Unlike the lively energy from before and the electric lights, the area was dark and wet. Kevin walked up to the path and looked down into the Sanctuary. The sign was ruined and had collapsed off to one side of the path. Darren stood across the road from the path.

"Kevin! Let's get out of here, man!"

"I just want to see."

"Let's fucking go, dude." Kevin ignored him and walked down the path a bit into the creek. Puddles of water stood around the concrete. Waterlogged rugs stood in the open. The metal grill was a pile of melted plastic and metal. The grass along the bank was charred black. Kevin felt his way around and then put on his phone light to look at the area. He ducked into one of the culverts but found that they had been cleaned out. Bits of glass and metal also lay on the ground and his shoes crunched over them. Darren found him and touched him on the back. He jumped a little.

"Just me, just me, dude, let's smoke and get the fuck out of here, they're gone, so's all this."

Kevin nodded and followed him up the path. The pair stepped into Darren's car. Darren opened up his center console and took out his bag of weed and some glass. "I'm too sober for this shit." He took a deep hit once he had loaded the bowl with a purple nug.

Kevin took a long hit and sat back in the seat and let it hold his body. Darren put in the key and was about to start the car when another car pulled up behind them. Darren let his hand go from the key and sat quietly looking at the car from the mirrors.

"Fuck, dude."

Kevin looked at the mirror. "Fuck."

Darren and Kevin both relaxed when two girls hopped out with a guy in the backseat. Kevin looked closely and saw Jenna.

"Shit, that's that girl and her friend."

Kevin opened the door and rolled out of the car and jogged over to them.

"Hey, hey," he said, walking up to Jenna and Amanda.

"O-M-G, you got out," Amanda said as Jenna hugged him around the shoulders. Jenna wiped a tear. "The cops got Dolph, he's in jail."

Kevin nodded. "That sucks. What are you guys doing here?"

"Just wanted to see what was left," Amanda said.

"Did you go down there for whatever?" Justin asked.

"Yeah. I didn't see anything. It's all broken or they just took it all," Kevin replied. Darren opened his door and walked over to the group.

Justin held up a hand. "Hey man."

Darren stood next to Kevin and crossed his arms. "You guys come back here?"

"Yeah, but it sounds like there's nothing."

"Look, dude it's like four, it's gonna be light soon and we need to get back."

"Yeah, we need to get home too. I have shit to do," Amanda said, pulling out her keys.

Jenna kissed Kevin right on the lips. "Text me, OK. I'm not going to sleep for awhile."

"Cool, I will."

Kevin and Darren broke away from the group and sat back down in the car. Darren started it and slowly pulled away from the neighborhood. Once he was back onto bigger roads he let the car open up and made it back to their neighborhood. He dropped Kevin off at the corner and Kevin rolled out. Darren rolled down the window. "Have a good night."

"Sure, you too."

Kevin shimmied back up to his window and back into his room. He stripped down and climbed into bed. He stared at the ceiling, his head resting on his tucked arm. He let the events of the night filter through his brain. His phone vibrated. He picked it up. Jenna texted him.

"Weren't you supposed to text me?"

Kevin replied. "Yeah, I forgot, I'm high af."

"I figured."

"Yeah, crazy night."

"Fuck the cops amiright?"

"Yeah, I had a good time, you know, earlier."

"Me too, you're pretty cute imho."

"Thanks, you're cute too."

"Alright, good. I'm falling asleep I think, tomorrow?"

"Sure."

Kevin let his phone drop onto the bed and let his mind drift to Jenna and the Sanctuary. He thought about what Dolph said about the suburbs. Kevin hadn't ever really thought about where he lived before. The houses did all look the same. On his block the same three houses repeated over and over again. The cars were boring sometimes. How many people did he know that got excited about a Nisscan Maxima? He thought about his own parents. They fought a little, they tried to hide it but he knew about it. He wondered how many other things went on that he had no idea about. Maybe the world wasn't all as nice as he thought. Was the Sanctuary real life? Was smoking and having a beer and getting laid real life? Were the suburbs just a clever cover for what people really wanted to do? Was the world he had known all fake? Was Dolph real? Was he right? Why was everyone afraid of drugs? And why do people always complain about noise? Like that time his Dad had to talk to the police about noise coming from their house. What was all this behind the clean cars and the tucked-in polo shirts. It was a mind fuck and Kevin didn't know what to do with it. His brain continued to think around this new mindfuck until he eventually drifted off to sleep.

The Ticket

Topher flicked the butt of his cigarette into the water off the concrete pier. He checked his watch for the time.

"Time to quit and go do paperwork," he said out loud to the breeze of the Seattle afternoon. The sky was covered in light clouds, letting a little bit of sun through.

He started walking away from the end of the pier and under the silent cranes towards the office to end his day. He filled out his required paperwork and clocked out. He replaced his card in the wall file and started walking out to his truck. He opened up the door. It squeaked loudly as usual and he climbed into the dusty cab covered with papers and food wrappers. He started the truck and looked at the gas gauge. It hovered below a quarter of a tank and he put the truck into gear. "Good thing payday is tomorrow," he thought. He drove over the tall West Seattle Bridge and threaded through Fauntleroy Street to a small apartment building. He pulled the truck to a stop and jumped out.

"Fuck this." He walked over to the passenger side and opened the door. He started to gather all the trash up from his truck and stuff it in plastic bags, stuffing the energy drink cans and other detritus into the sacks until he came across an unscratched Washington state lottery ticket.

Topher pulled out a coin from his stash in the ashtray and started to scratch. He put the weight of his body on one hip as he scratched the ticket.

All the symbols matched. He looked on the back of the ticket and re-read the rules. He read them again and looked at the front of the ticket. He looked at the back of the ticket and a chill ran down his body. He turned the ticket over and looked at the front again.

"Prize: $50,000 with bonus symbol! Match all 4 to win!"

Topher looked around. He pocketed the ticket in a swift motion and closed the truck door. He carried the garbage over to the dumpster behind the squat apartment building and threw the bags over the top. He touched his pocket again to make sure the ticket was still in his pocket. He would have to try the ticket to make sure he was right. He walked back to the truck and hopped up into the cab and drove four blocks over to the small corner shop. The shop stood next to a busy bar. He parked on the street and walked into the shop. He stood at the counter.

"Topher!" A short man with a thick Middle Eastern accent walked out carrying a pile of boxes. "I stock, always stock."

"How's business, Ahmed?"

"Good, very good, very business."

"Hey, can you try this ticket out for me? I think it's a winner."

"Sure, sure."

Ahmed took the ticket that Topher offered him and he scanned it under the large green machine. The lights on the digital display started flashing.

"You're a big winner, man!" Ahmed said with a broad smile. "You won the big prize, fifty!"

Topher's mouth dropped open. "No shit?"

"Machine knows the codes, you won fifty thousand!" Ahmed turned the ticket over and looked at the back. "You have to go to Olympia to turn this in - it looks like you have until today," he said, looking at the ticket.

"Today?"

"Yeah, there's a deadline from sale - ninety days, it says the date right here." Ahmed pointed at the date stamp.

Topher grabbed at his own face. "Fuck me, I don't have gas to get down there today."

Ahmed shrugged his shoulders. "Ask some friends - you can pay them back when you get the money."

"Fuck, I don't even know how to call."

Ahmed shrugged his shoulders. "Try the train."

Topher nodded his head. " I can make the train station."

"Good luck!" Ahmed said, smiling.

Topher walked out to his truck and slid into the seat. He started driving to the Sounder station. He drove out of West Seattle and passed over the tall bridge and turned off at the 1st street exit and started driving into downtown. The traffic was already starting to pick up and he zig zagged around on the street grid to avoid the back up until he finally pulled into the historic Pioneer Square neighborhood with its tall trees and pleasant store fronts. The electric buses and their overhead lines whizzed by. Topher found a parking spot for his truck and he pulled into it. He put the truck in park and started to dig around his seats for change. He checked his wallet for money. He found $3 and he kept finding change. He even found a dollar under the passenger seat. Soon he had gathered the $6 for the fare and walked into the station. He walked up to the small booth with his bills and change.

"One ticket to Lakewood please." He flashed a toothy smile.

"Here you are." She put his ticket under the thick glass.

"Thanks."

"Track 2, ten minutes."

"Yeah." Topher walked out to track 2 and waited for the large commuter train to arrive. He jiggled his pockets. The leftover change had to get him from Lakewood to Olympia. Topher watched the rails for the train to come in. He realized that he had no plan to get home. The ticket money wouldn't be in cash, most likely, and he was probably spending the night in Olympia until he could figure out how to get back. He touched his wallet in the back of his pants again to make sure it was still there. He looked down the rails again and then started to think about what to do with the money. He realized that he didn't really know what to do with that much money. Maybe a new truck? But maybe it was an opportunity too. Maybe he could do something for himself with the money. Should he go to college? For what? What was he good at besides driving machines and construction?

The train finally pulled into the station and Topher waited for all the passengers to depart before stepping into the train himself. He walked upstairs to the second level and sat down in the corner. He looked out towards the derelict warehouses and spots of new growth that dotted the area. Every block seemed to be a mixture of cannabis shops, food, and random stores all dominated by the large Starbucks headquarters. Topher waited for the train to leave and wondered how long it took for a train to get out of the station. Another fifteen minutes passed before the train finally left the station. It pulled away from the platform and wound its way through the train yard and out of West Seattle. The train passed under the West Seattle bridge at a good speed and then out onto the rails.

According to the guide, the next stop would be in Tukwila. The train pulled in. The second level wasn't filled with passengers. Topher only saw a couple of other people. The other passengers were all listening to something on their phones. Topher didn't really ever do that but he decided to try it out. He pulled out his ear buds from his pocket. He blew off some work dust from them and put them in. At Tukwila, more people got on and a few of them filtered into the second level of his car.

Topher noticed her immediately. She was pretty, had curly red hair and carried a big bag. With her phone out and ear buds in, she walked up to the second level of the car and picked out a seat three rows up from him. He looked over the top of his phone to look at her again. She put down her bag and slid it along the floor until it was between her feet.

The train departed the station at Tukwila and proceeded to its next stop in Kent. Topher listened to music and watched the woman in front of him. The distance from Tukwila and Kent was not far and the train soon pulled into the next station. The woman didn't move. The train moved on to its next station at Auburn.

Topher looked out the window and noticed that the train was slowing down and moved around some curves before violently coming to a stop. The jolt threw him from his relaxed position on his seat. He splayed all over the floor. The other passengers tried to brace themselves but without success. Topher lifted up his head and tried to get his bearings. He stood up and looked around. He took out his headphones. The lady he had kept his eye on rushed over to him.

"Sir? Sir, are you alright?"

Topher looked around in a daze. "Yeah, I think so." He wobbled a bit and he sat back down on his chair.

She sat in front of him. "Look in my eyes." Topher looked her right in the eye. "How many fingers?"

Topher looked at her hand. "Four."

"Good. Any ringing in your ears?"

"No, maybe a little. Might have hit my head."

"Mild concussion maybe." She stood up and got her bag. "Have some water."

Topher drank from her bottle. An announcement soon came

over the train.

"Ladies and Gentlemen, we apologize for the jolt, there has been a landslide on the track but the train is operational, we will be returning to the Kent Station."

There was an audible groan from the passengers. Topher leaned back in his seat. She returned to the seat near him.

"This train is so unreliable. I should just drive it and be done with it. I'm Jeanine, you?"

Topher lifted up his head. "Topher."

"Is that short for something?"

"Christopher, like the guy on That 70's Show."

"That's funny," she said, tucking her bag under her feet again.

Topher checked himself to make sure he still had his phone and his wallet. He checked his wallet to make sure he still had the ticket.

"Well, I'm fucked."

"Why?" Jeanine asked.

"I have to get to Olympia by 5."

"They usually send buses to get everyone to the other stations. It takes a while but it gets the job done."

"Yeah, but I'm not going to make it."

Jeanine drank from the water bottle herself. The train jerked and started to move backwards slowly.

"What's in Olympia?"

"Just, uh, I have to visit a government office."

"How are you feeling? Dizziness?"

"Are you a nurse or something?"

"Close. Physician's assistant."

"That's why you keep asking me why I'm alright."

"Yeah. Falls can be bad if they aren't taken care of. I don't think you hit your head, though. May I?" She leaned forward and felt around his head for any bumps.

"No bumps or lumps, I think you'll be OK."

"Thanks." Topher shook his head a little bit to get his bearings back. He opened his phone and tried to figure out how to get to Lakewood from Kent and then try to figure out how to make it to that office. Jeanine didn't move. She looked out the window and into the cloudy day.

"Why do you have to get to Olympia so bad? Legal thing?"

"No, no, I'm not, uh, a con or anything. I had some juvie stuff but, uh, I've been a good guy."

"Ah." Jeanine said. The train kept moving slowly until the Kent station pulled into view and the train stopped. Topher stood up and waited for her to follow.

"Thanks for looking after me."

"Sure, it's my job."

"Are you going to wait for a bus?"

"Probably not," she replied. "I'm going to skip it and get an Uber to Lakewood, that's where my car is, anyway."

"Alright, well thanks." Topher started to walk off the train. He ducked his head down to get down the stairs. Jeanine followed him and he looked around the platform. Sound Transit officials stood around the platform. Jeanine touched his arm.

"Listen, you must need to get where you're going, why don't you share an Uber with me? You seem nice enough and it'll at least get you to Lakewood."

Topher shuffled his feet. "I mean, I would, and thank you but I, uh. It's Thursday and maybe I should just wait for the bus."

Jeanine smiled. "Don't get paid until tomorrow?"

Topher stood up taller. "Yeah, I don't want to take advantage of anybody or anything. I'm not a beggar."

Jeanine smiled. "Come on. They'll be hours figuring this out. Come with me, car will be here in like ten minutes and I'll get you on your way."

Topher followed her out of the station and to the little drive outside of it. Jeanine looked down at her phone and waited for the car to arrive.

"You don't have to help me," Topher remarked.

"I know, but I want to." Jeanine smiled and looked around the area waiting for her car.

"I'm just not used to, you know, taking help, this whole thing is just weird, weird day."

"Yeah, it's one of those days that needs to end with a nice glass of wine at a bar." Jeanine checked her phone again.

"You work in Seattle?" Topher asked.

Jeanine nodded. "I do, at a clinic for low income clients."

"Ah, cool, I bet you help a lot of people."

"I try to, what about you?"

"Port of Seattle."

"Nice. I bet that's a good job."

"Pays the bills, not much else, unless I get overtime."

"Sure. Oh look, this Prius, this is us."

A black car pulled up to the curb. He rolled down the window. "Jeanine?" he asked.

"That's us!" she replied.

Topher climbed into the front seat and Jeanine slid into the back seat. The driver started off for the Lakewood train station. He drove onto I-5 and got up to speed just in time to slow down for traffic. A light drizzle started to fall and dotted the windshield with droplets. The car crept forward until they passed the Emerald Queen Casino. Its bright sign announced new tribute bands that were coming to play and their latest employment openings.

The traffic cleared and the driver sped up again. Topher stayed quiet as the car pressed through the traffic towards Lakewood. The car wound around the curves of the highway and past exits until the driver finally pulled off at Bridgeport Boulevard and drove up the Pacific Highway to the large parking garage. He pulled into the station and stopped.

"Here we are," he said in a thick Arab accent.

"Thanks!" Jeanine said. "Five stars."

"Thank you!" he said. He pulled away slowly once both of them were out of the car.

"Alright, I'm curious," Jeanine said, hefting her bag over her shoulder. "Why do you need to get to Olympia? Really?"

Topher looked up and over her head. "I got a scratch ticket, for a lot of money and if I don't turn it in today, I don't win."

"Is that all?"

"Yup, I just didn't have the gas to get to Olympia in my truck so I thought I'd take the train and now I have to hope for this bus."

"How are you getting home?" Jeanine asked, touching his arm.

"No clue. Probably sleep in the bus station until morning. I think I have enough change to get at least up here."

Jeanine tilted her head in thought for a moment. "Let's go."

Topher rubbed his chin. "What?"

"Let's go - Oly isn't that far from here, we can get you there in time and get you back home."

Topher stepped back. "You've been too nice to me, I can't, I can't take any more generosity, you've been too nice to me and we just met on that train and I, I'll just have to figure it out."

"You have figured it out. You met a nice lady on a train who against the advice of public safety experts is going to drive a man to Oly. Come on, my car is on level four."

"Why are you being so nice to me?" Topher's voice edged the words.

Jeanine pondered it for a moment. "You deserve that money and I'm going to see that you get it. If it makes you feel better you can pay me when you cash the check. Here." Jeanine opened her wallet and passed him her business card. "You seem honest and if you were planning something terrible you would have already done it or you're the slowest creeper I know."

Topher took the card. It was printed on expensive paper. The name of the clinic was neatly printed on the top of the card. Her name, Jeanine Gatling, was printed in the middle of the card.

"I don't have a card but my full name is Christopher Sullivan. I can prove it." Topher pulled out his badge from his wallet for the Port of Seattle. Jeanine took the card from him. His picture looked just like him and his name stood out in bold letters. The green and blue logo for the Port of Seattle was in the right corner. "You can call the union too. I'm a member."

"See, now, come on, if we're going to make it there before they close we need to go." Jeanine turned on her heel and started walking to her car. Topher followed her. She opened the trunk with her key and slid her bag into it. She pulled out a smaller bag from it and closed the trunk on the beige Camry.

"You can slide the seat back, you have long legs!" she said, opening the driver's side door.

Topher opened the door and looked for the controls.

"It's right here." She pulled up a metal bar and the chair slid back. Topher manoeuvered himself into the seat. Jenine pulled out her phone. "What's the address?"

Topher pulled out his wallet from the back of his pants. He took out the ticket and showed it to her. Jeanine put the address into the GPs and slid it into a holder on her dash.

"Thirty five minutes, plenty of time. Let's get moving." She started the car and pulled out of the big parking garage and waited for space to turn onto Pacific Highway. They passed the used car lots and gas stations and soon pulled onto I-5 just before the big military base. She brought the car up to speed and they started the trip to Olympia.

Topher rubbed his chin again and looked out the window. "I can't thank you enough for, you know, helping me."

"I want to," Jeanine replied.

The pair sat in silence and let a few miles pass. Lakewood ended and they entered the bit of empty land between Tacoma and Olympia.

"So, what are you going to do with the money?" Jeanine asked. "You don't have to tell me, you know, I just figured you had plans."

Topher took a deep breath. "I honestly don't know, maybe a new truck but then I thought maybe I should go back to school but I don't know what or how I'd even do that."

"What did you want to do in highschool?" Jeanine asked passing a truck in the middle lane of the highway.

"Not be in highschool!" Topher said with a chuckle. "Parents didn't have much, so I wanted to work from a pretty young age. Have my own money, you know."

"I hear that from my clients at the clinic a lot. Many of them didn't even graduate."

"I dropped out in 11th grade. Took the GED and started working in restaurants, then driving truck, worked construction, concrete, all that good stuff."

"And now at the Port of Seattle."

"Yeah, yeah, it's a good job."

"And union."

"It is."

"But maybe you want to do something else?"

"Yeah, maybe, I think that'd be cool. I bet you went to college and all that."

Jeanine nodded her head. "I did."

Topher nodded his head. The car fell silent as the miles rolled away.

"Thurston county.," Jeanine said pointing out the sign with her delicate hand.

"Almost there," Topher said.

"Are you feeling anything from hitting your head on the train?" Jeanine asked.

"No, I'm OK, not my first time."

"Good, just keeping an eye on a concussion."

"OK."

Jeanine looked to the GPs to see where to turn off and she took an exit marked "Capitol." She drove around the streets of Olympia until they found the Washington State Gaming office.

"We're here. Let's go get your money."

Topher opened the door. "You don't have to come in with me, I mean, you've already taken time out of your day and I don't want to bother you."

Jeanine shook her head. "I'm already on this little adventure. Let's go."

The pair walked into the office. Topher walked up to the desk.

"Hi, um. I'm just here to turn this in."

Topher took the ticket out of his pocket and put it on the counter. The lady took it from him and scanned the barcode.

"Congratulations, it looks like you've won $50,000 from the Washington state lottery."

Topher glanced over at Jeanine. She flashed him a smile.

"If you give me a few moments I'll get the paperwork and get you your check." Topher nodded.

Topher turned to Jeanine. "I guess there's paperwork."

"There always is." Jeanine and Topher waited for several minutes until the desk person returned. She shoved her glasses up on her nose and put the paperwork down on the desk.

"Please fill out your name, address on this. Behind here is your winnings, the amount of taxes deducted and your final amount. Sign at the bottom and I'll get your check cut right now."

Topher took the pen she offered and slowly filled out the forms and signed the bottom.

He pushed the paperwork back towards her.

"Thanks," she replied. She checked over the forms and started to input all the information into the computer. In a few moments she returned with an envelope.

"Here you are Mr. Sullivan, your winnings. Thanks for playing."

Topher took the envelope and nodded at the woman. "Thanks."

Jeanine touched his arm. "How does it feel?"

"I don't know, I guess it's not quite real yet."

"You need to get that in the bank right away. Who do you bank with?"

"Um, Chase."

"There's probably a branch of that around here. We should put it in right away and then we'll have to get you back to Seattle."

Topher looked at the envelope. He didn't open it to reveal its contents. He just looked at it. He turned it over in his hands.

"Come on, let's go out to the car."

Jeanine started for the car with Topher in tow.She found a branch of the bank in Olympia. She guided the car down State Street through the old downtown and towards the bank. She sent Topher in to deposit his check. Topher walked into the bank and deposited the check after filling out what seemed like endless forms. Topher filled each one out carefully and after forty five minutes of standing in the bank the check was deposited into his savings account and Topher was officially richer by $41,285.34.

Topher walked back out to Jeanine waiting in the car.

" I was about to come find you!" Jeanine said, starting the car.

"Just a lot of paperwork,Topher said.

"Let's celebrate - why don't we go to the bar over there and have a drink," Jeanine said, pointing out a pleasant restaurant.

Topher held up his hands. "There's a hold on it. I just have my bus fare."

"Thanks. OK,, you can pay me back if you want. Let's have a drink - we deserve it after the day we've had. Come on."

Jeanine stepped out of the car and left it parked where it was. The pair walked over to the bar. They walked into the wood paneled space. The bar and restaurant were filled with historic pictures of the bar. Jeanine asked for a table for two, somewhere quiet.

Topher sat across from her and the waitress brought them drinks. Jeanine sipped on her martini and Topher took a drink from his beer.

"I think you should use that money for school," she said leaning into the booth.

"I thought about that but guys like me don't go to school."

"Oh that's not true at all," Jeanine said, drinking from her Martini again.

"What would I even go to school for anyway?"

"You could learn to code. There's good money and it's in demand."

Topher drank from his beer. "Yeah, I guess I could. I've gotten pretty handy with computers at work."

"And you won't have to be outside all the time in the rain." She pointed outside where another rain storm had begun to fall, turning the streets into a glossy reflection of the light from the shops.

"Don't just buy another truck," Jeanine said. " Just my ideas, I guess. I don't mean to tell you what to do or anything."

Topher smiled a bit. "I kinda like it, you look out for me. It's been a long time since I've had someone looking out for me."

"I know that feeling. It's been ages since I've been on a date."

Topher's brow raised. "You're a nice woman and pretty. Come down to the Port, there's five guys who'd be the first to ask you out."

Jeanine laughed. "I might have to try that. What about you? Would you ask me out?"

Topher sipped his beer. "That's not what I meant, I mean, I didn't mean to come on to you."

"I want you to."

Topher reached across the table and took her hand. "Alright."

The pair ordered their food from the pleasant waitress. They ate together and finished their drinks.

Jeanine had a glass of water before she paid the bill and they walked out of the restaurant. The pair stood under the awning outside the bar.

Jeanine scrunched her shoulders. "It's chilly, I shouldn't have left my jacket in the car."

"Let's run for it," Topher suggested. The pair ran over to her car and she unlocked the doors as she jogged. They slipped into the car and took a deep breath.

"Let's get some heat going and dry out." She turned on the car and turned the heat on high.

"I'm ready for the drive back to Seattle, ready?"

"You really want to do that?"

"If you'll let me."

Topher looked into her eyes. "I don't…" His voice trailed off.

"You're not taking advantage of me."

"I want to kiss you." Topher let out.

"Then kiss me."

Topher leaned over to the driver's side and planted a kiss on her lips. She opened her mouth and the kiss stayed longer than he intended. They finally broke the kiss.

"Are you ready to go now?"

Topher reached for her hand. "Yeah. Let's go."

"By the way, you can call me Jeannie."

"Okay Jeannie. Thank you, for everything. I've never had someone be this nice to me."

"I figured that out. I hope I can keep being nice to you."

"I'd like that," Topher said, holding up her hand. Her hand felt soft and nice against his rough working man's hands.

Jeanine took her hand away and started driving back to Seattle over the wet highway. They threaded their way back to the Seattle Sounder station and her car rolled to a stop. Topher picked up her phone and put in his number.

"Call me," she said.

"I will. I don't want you to leave."

"Kiss me, then."

Topher leaned over and kissed her again. The glow of the station lights illuminated the pair and Jeanine put her arm on his shoulder and hugged him as close as she could bring his body to her. They broke the embrace and Jeanine leaned back. "You're a good kisser, Topher."

"You're not too bad yourself."

"I should go," she said.

"I'll call you tomorrow."

"Alright, Mr. Sullivan. Thank you for the adventure."

Topher looked down at the carpeted floor. "Thank you again for everything."

He took a deep breath and opened the door of her car and stepped out. He turned around and watched her pull away from the station and out onto the road. The raindrops splashed on his shoulders until he started walking to his truck.

The RKO Killer

Farben sat on the stairs tying his shoes. He stood up and moved through the short foyer of his apartment towards the kitchen. The smell of breakfast floated through the air. He opened the pocket doors revealing Mrs. Fowler hard at work on the stove in the kitchen. Farben slid into the breakfast nook. A thoughtful gaze through the window revealed the sun was muted by the morning clouds, on the move from the familiar wind of the Windy City.

"Good morning, Isaac," Anne said, smiling.

Farben lit a cigarette. "I'm going down KYW today."

"Yes I know, I'm very well aware of your appointments, Isaac. After all, I make your schedule." Anna looked over her shoulders as she flipped a pancake. "I saw a radio down at Marshall Fields the other day. I think we might get one, pay on time." Anna said. She turned her head to see her husband coming into the kitchen. Mr. Fowler wiped his hands on his apron as he entered from the servant's stairway.

"How's the car, Mr. Fowler?" Farben asked over the morning newspaper.

"Good, Mr. Farben, it is ready for your meeting downtown at Commonwealth Edison. Czarek is a great guy, really smart and his English is improving!" Rustin said with a broad smile.

"Maybe I'll get a radio for the parlor," Farben spoke aloud

while looking at a Marshall Fields ad for the new appliance.

Mrs. Fowler put breakfast down in front of him. Farben folded the newspaper and put it on the table. He put out his cigarette and ate quickly. He glanced at the paper a few more times before standing up from the breakfast nook.

"Are you ready to go, Rustin? The radio doesn't wait for anyone from what I've heard." If Farben was going into the radio business, he thought that he probably should really buy a radio.

He put on his coat and hat and rode the elevator down to the shimmering art deco lobby below. His shoes clicked on the marble floors as he strode across the lobby. The bright-faced black doorman opened the door.

"Good Morning, Mr. Farben. Have a good day!"

Isaac smiled at him, tipped his hat and looked down the street for Mr. Fowler and the car. A line of cars paraded by and finally Czarek pulled up. The doorman opened the door and Farben and Rustin stepped into the back of the car. Czarek put the car in gear and moved the car out into the traffic.

"Now, 72 West Adams, the Commonwealth Edison building. I'm sure there is a large sign for KYW," Farben said.

Czarek piloted the car towards the radio station and came to a stop beneath its turn of the century facade. The Marque out front read, "Commonwealth Edison."

Farben opened his own door and looked up at the building as he removed his hat and moved through the rotating doors into the building. The lobby of the Commonwealth Edison building was more modern than its 1900 facade. The beautiful aluminum information and telephone desk stood gleaming in the corner. The floor was clean and tiled with white and turquoise tiles. In the center of the lobby the floor read, "Commonwealth Edison" and a large light bulb in yellow tiles. People hurried in and out of the building on the cloudy Tuesday morning. Farben went to the floor directory and looked for the KYW radio station and proceeded over to the bank of gleaming bronze elevators.

"12th Floor please."

The car attendant, a boy of about twelve or thirteen dressed in a neat uniform, smiled and started the car with a tug of a lever.

"Going all the way up sir!" A few minutes later the elevator doors opened. "12th floor sir!"

The elevators opened to a hall of wooden and glass doors and dividers. Farben looked left and right and then chose to go left when he saw a door embossed with the letters KYW Offices. Farben walked in and addressed the secretary.

"Good Morning. My name is Isaac Farben, this is my associate Rustin Fowler, we are here to see a Mr. Searlye, Daniel Searlye."

The receptionist smiled and left her desk. Farben wrote down his number on her stenographers' pad. She came back to the desk. She looked down and saw the number. She rapidly tore off the paper, smiled and put it in her bra. Rustin shot him a disapproving look. Farben looked towards the door and smiled.

"Mr. Searlye will see you now," she said, opening the paneled door. Farben crossed the short distance and walked into the office, dominated by a large wooden desk with clean art deco lines.

"Isaac! Come in! Sit down!"

"Good to see you too, Daniel. Got a light?" Farben said, holding out a cigarette.

Daniel pointed towards the large lighter. Farben flicked the mechanism and lit his cigarette.

"How are you doing? We haven't seen you around the club much these days."

"I don't go often, you know that. It's the German-American club. I wouldn't be a member at all if my father didn't insist on keeping it up all the time." Rustin secreted himself on a simple chair in the corner and placed his hat in his lap.

"Ah, well, I see, uh, well some of the guys have been bringing their own liquor, you should drop in sometime and try it. The guys from the war would like to see you, I'm sure," he said.

Farben looked out the window onto the Chicago skyline.

"I'll see about it. I'm sure you didn't ask me down here to talk about the club."

"No, I did not, sadly. But I know you can solve it. It's about one of our radio performers. She, well, she disappeared. And we don't know where either. We think it might have to do with a guy we hired into to help with the sound effects. He was convicted of public fighting and put in the pen for biting a man's neck and disfiguring him. He took a shine to her. This is all rumored of course. Her next show is Friday night."

"It's Tuesday," Farben said coolly.

"Exactly! I need for you to find her and do so quietly."

At that moment his phone rang. He answered it.

"Yes, yes, what? How do you know that? Did you call his house? No answer? Did you go over there? Did you call the police? Good. OK, I'll handle this with our man."

He replaced the receiver.

"More work for you, I'm afraid. I need you to find a man. He has been a sensation of radio in southern Illinois and we want him up here at KYW but I can't find him to get him the offer so I need you to go down to Champagne and find this man. I want him on radio!"

"I see. What do you know about him?"

"I knew you'd ask. I have something, a file, around here somewhere." He shuffled through some papers. "Ah ha, here it is." He produced a small leather folio with a collection of articles and a mug shot.

"Here is our man."

I.G Farben looked over the pictures and a few police reports.

The report read: "Freddie Weeks, born 1897, no known place of birth, no known family."

Farben took the file from Daniel and waved Rustin over.

"He robbed a bank in Hannibal, MO and also asked out the teller apparently. And he broke into a house and robbed the family but then read a story to the children to help them sleep after the invasion. His most recent crime, the assault and battery, took place at an illegal bar in June 1925 where he bludgeoned a man over the head with a whiskey bottle and then cut him several times with the broken glass and performed, it says here, lewd acts to the victim's face. He bled out there on the floor. This guy is a strange criminal for sure, and you want me to go to Champagne, find him and get him back to Chicago for radio while he is on the run. The police won't be happy, that's for sure."

"Don't worry about the police, I.G. They are going to get their reward after. Once he has done a story telling bit on the radio they can break into the building and capture him live on air."

"How dramatic."

"Exactly - it will definitely sell radios. People won't want to miss out on this kind of drama ever again!"

"We won't be either, apparently, although I'm sure my secretary will be sitting at home glued to the radio listening to the whole thing. What do you want us to do about your missing performer?"

"Nevermind about her, I'll put someone less competent on that. This is much more important."

Rustin shook his head, "We'll get right on it." Farben looked at Rustin with a raised eyebrow. "This isn't a gum-shoe investigation in a dime novel!" Farben thought. Rustin was new and had much to learn. The men left the office shortly after, file in hand. I.G. Farben left the Commonwealth Edison building and looked around the sidewalk for where Czarek had parked. He didn't see Czarek or the car anywhere nearby. Farben was just about to step inside to call in a booth when Czarek and the car finally arrived. Farben stepped out into the dusty street to get into the car.

"Sorry, getting lunch!" Czarek replied.

Czarek opened the back door for Farben and Rustin. Rustin and Isaac stepped into the back of the Packard and they sped off into afternoon Chicago traffic. Farben soon arrived at the office. The elevator took them up to the 8th floor of the fashionable Madison Building.

Farben settled in to the small library behind the desk. He laid out the information. He looked around the room for a road atlas of the United States. Finding one, he looked at where the crimes took place on the map and at any relevant roads in the area. He stepped out in the office, map in hand.

"Where is Rustin?"

"He is downstairs dealing with a tenant. Do you want me to get him?"

"Please."

Rustin arrived shortly after in the small room.

"Yessir?"

"We need to plan a route to Champagne, just you and me."

"There are some good roads to get to Champagne, mostly country. Do you know if US 45 is done yet?" Farben said looking at the map.

"I think it is. According to this it's supposed to be done December, 1924. That's a good sign," Rustin said, tracing it with his finger.

"Sounds good I bet there are some country roads we can get around if the highway isn't fully open or blocked," Farben said looking at the tiny red lines on the paper.

"I think so. We'll leave in the morning. Pack your bags, I should take all day to get there if not longer. And then we have to start looking, in earnest."

The next morning. Farben came down for breakfast. His bag was packed. He set it by the stairs. He had a few more things to gather. As he made his way to the kitchen. he could hear Anna crying.

"I'm so sorry Rustin....I'm so sorry. I would die to give you a child!"

Farben stayed in the Foyer for a minute.

"Anna, I love you. We'll have a baby when God decides. It's alright, really, I promise. We'll have some fun when I get back from this trip with Isaac."

She sniffed, "OK."

Farben walked over to the stairs and pounded his foot on the last stair, shouting, "Good morning!"

He walked over towards the kitchen and breakfast nook just as the two quickly separated.

"Here's your breakfast, Isaac," Anna said, wiping her face.

"Thanks, something wrong?" he said as she planted a plate of bacon, eggs, toast and fruit in front of him.

"No, no, just the smoke from the stove. I'll open a window."

"Are you ready, Rustin?"

"Yes sir."

Farben rode the elevator down to the ground floor with Rustin. The men walked together out to the Packard sedan sitting in the parking lot alongside the building. Rustin slid into the driver's seat and Farben ensconced himself in the back with the morning paper. Rustin pulled out into traffic and winding his way through the Chicago streets finally made it out onto Highway 45. The car rumbled down the newly paved road. A few small signs announced the towns along the way. Farben spotted a sign for Champagne. The Highway wasn't that busy and Rustin honked at other cars making their way up the US highway towards Chicago. Two hours into the drive, right before Champagne, Rustin pulled into a small gas station. Both men got out to stretch their legs and get some cigarettes in the small store. Farben picked out three packs of Murad Turkish cigarettes, one for Rustin, two for himself, paid for them along with two iced Coca-Cola sodas and met Rustin outside. Farben leaned against the car and offered him the pack while lighting one himself.

"I heard what you were talking about with Anna this morning."

"Oh, I'm sorry. We were just hoping we had done it this time."

"That time of the month?"

"Unfortunately, especially for a woman who wants to get pregnant."

Farben shrugged "I'm sorry Rustin, I didn't even know you two were trying. My mother will give that child everything just to have a baby to dote on."

Rustin chuckled. "Do you ever want kids?"

Farben looked around. "Not really. Don't want to get married either. That's my brother's job."

"It's not so bad."

"What?"

"Married life might help you with your problems."

Farben laughed, shaking his head as he flicked his cigarette into the dirt, "I already have a nice lady who cooks my meals and takes care of me. I think Anna is enough wife for the both of us."

Rustin laughed, "You are right about that."

Farben opened the front of the Packard and sat in the front. Rustin pulled out and back onto the highway. Two hours later they arrived in Champagne.

"Let's go take a look around - supposedly, he robbed the bank at Main St. and Market," Farben indicated on a map of the town. He navigated as Rustin guided the car. They passed the University of Illinois and worked their way through the streets past pleasant homes. Rustin pulled up to the First Bank of Champagne-Urbana and parked. Then they walked into the bank and inquired at the teller desk about the robbery. The bank was of older build, with some short columns out front and large brass doors that led onto a stone floor, and metal bars surrounding the tellers and the wealth they doled out to account holders.

"Were you here the day of the robbery?"

"Yessir. I was, it was horrible."

"Is the President of the bank here?"

"Yessir, I'll get him for you." She closed the cage and moved towards the back of the bank.

"Good afternoon, Mr. Farben." A short rotund man approached Farben in the lobby of the bank with an outstretched hand.

"Good afternoon."

"Miles, my name is Richard Miles."

"Mr. Miles, I was just inquiring about your robbery last week."

"Oh, I see. Were you planning on opening an account? We're insured, of course."

"No, not at this time. My partner and I just drove down from Chicago and we're looking into the local robbery. We're actually looking for the robber."

"Ah, I see. While we would like to have someone with your name with funds on deposit, I understand. Yes, he held up the bank. Police efforts to find him haven't turned anything up, unfortunately."

"Have you heard anything about his whereabouts?" Rustin said.

"Not lately. There was a rumor going around the girls in the office that he was still in the area." He leaned in. "They find him very attractive and that photo in the newspaper only made it worse."

"Ah ha. Did the newspaper have a name?"

"Yes. Freddie Weeks, I guess he's a known criminal with quite a rap sheet!"

"Thank you for your time, Mr. Miles."

Rustin and Farben left the bank and walked back out. Farben lit a cigarette and leaned against the side of the car.

"Looks like the guy is still nearby," Rustin said.

"It would appear."

"What's next?"

"If I were a known criminal, I would hide outside of town, but I would need to come into town for supplies from time to time and maybe try to find some hootch or a girl."

"It's not going to be that easy to find the local speakeasies around here - things are probably quiet and he may not need female companionship if he is just stealing." Rustin said with a shrug.

Farben smiled. "That's where being a Farben may help. Let's find ourselves a place to stay."

The men both got back into the car and Rustin drove around the area until they found a nice looking brick and wood motel called "The Champagne Inn." The vacancy sign was lit. Rustin pulled into the parking lot; Farben inquired for a room and came out with two keys.

"Here's yours. We're room 212." Farben offered him the small key. They walked up the carpeted staircase. The white painted door revealed a simple room. The white metal frame beds dominated the space. A bureau with a mirror stood against another wall with a sink that stuck out of the wall. Two glasses stood on the bureau. A towel rack by the cold water sink held two simple cotton towels.

The men put their bags away. Rustin stood up from the bed. "I'm going to go call Anna - she's going to be wondering about us."

"Of course. I'm going to inquire about the local happenings."

Farben walked down the stairs to the front desk. He smiled at the clerk, a young man with a white shirt, bow tie, and a pleasant face who put aside his paper.

"Mr. Farben! How can I help you! Is everything alright? We're very happy to have you staying with us."

"My friend and I were wondering what there was to do in this town. You know, anything we should see."

"If you gentlemen are looking for places to socialize, there is Martell's Pharmacy - it's a soda fountain. People like to go there. You also might try Young's Place."

"Ah, what do they do at Young's Place?"

The clerk leaned over the counter. "It's a jazz club for people about town but they serve alcohol."

"Ah. How does one get in?"

He looked around the lobby, "You go and pay the doorman 20 cents and say, 'It's cold in December.' He'll let you know how to get served."

"Thank you very much."

"Anything else, Mr. Farben?"

"Do you have an evening paper here?"

"The News-Gazette is the afternoon paper and the Courier is the morning paper. Both are on the table there."

"Thank you." Farben sidled over to the table where the papers were displayed and looked at the headlines. Farben grabbed both papers and waited for Rustin to come back from the telephone booth.

"How's Anna?"

"Fine, fine, glad we're here."

"Good, let's talk to the local grocers. They might have seen him. He is always mentioned as working alone, so I doubt that he would send someone to get supplies."

Rustin and Farben headed out to the Packard. Farben pointed out a few local grocers from the newspapers. He started his inquiries at the smaller places including a self-serve operation on the south end of the town, but didn't turn up anything definitive. Most of the men recognized him from the picture in the News-Gazette, but not for being in their store at any time. Farben watched the sun go down on the rising fields as he thought about where to turn next. It was time to make their way to Young's Place. Farben was out of the car as soon as Rustin parked it. He went up to the doorman and paid him $1 and said the words.

"When you sit down and the waitress asks for your order, just say you'll have a glass of ice water with extra ice and she'll bring you the county's finest whiskey."

"Thanks."

The place looked like a furniture store had left its odds and ends at the club. The stage was small and the bar was a glass and wood affair over which signs for various sugary drinks were prominently displayed. A black woman stood on the stage in a red dress in the modern flapper style with tassels on the hem singing a sad song. The club was only half filled. Farben and Rustin sat at a small table.

The pleasant-faced waitress came over and leaned down towards the men.

"What'll it be, boys?"

"Two glasses of ice water with ice."

"Will that be all?" She looked seductively at Rustin.

"I'm married," he said, meeting her gaze.

"I don't see your wife here."

"Trust me, gal, he's married, we'll just get those drinks."

"If y'all want to party later you just let me know! Drinks coming right up, boys."

"And now we wait," Rustin said.

"Exactly."

The waitress returned with a smile and the requisite drinks. The men sipped the harsh moonshine and kept an eye out for their quarry.

"So what exactly should we be listening for?"

"Anything of course, any clues or hints."

"I'm going to work the room," Rustin said. He stood up with his glass and started walking around the tables. He eventually settled at a poker game and plunked down a dollar and the dealer dealt him in. Farben looked around to see if anyone was talking about the case. He decided to try the bartender. The mirror and woodwork was oval and as Anna would put it, "last century." It was masculine, and held quite a bit of stock. The wood on the back matched the deep reddish brown of the bar, accentuated with brass work along the bottom edge for boots and at the ends.

"Evening, barkeep."

"Evening." He kept pouring more drinks and putting them on the bar for the serving girl to pick up.

"You hear about the bank robber in town?"

"Everyone has," he said, wiping the bar down.

"Yeah, I'm looking for him. I have a deal for him."

The barkeep leaned on the bar. "I've never seen him but I hear he comes from the north with the trucks. He could be hiding anywhere along the highway. There's abandoned houses and farms out there. If I were a criminal that's where I'd hide."

"That's helpful. Thanks." The barkeep looked down at the bar. Farben left 50 cents and turned to collect Rustin.

He negotiated his way over to the poker table where Rustin was sitting. From the looks of his pile, he was removing the players' money almost directly from their pockets. Farben squeezed his shoulder. The hand concluded and Rustin cashed out of the game and stuffed the fistful of dollars and coins into his jacket pocket. The pair headed outside into the crisp Illinois night air. At moments, their breath created small puffs of steam. The pair began to walk back to the car which was parked a few streets away. The journey was halfway completed when three drunk men shouted them down with slurred words.

"That fucker there took my fucking money!"

Rustin and Farben turned around to see the motley group, who were clearly intoxicated.

"It was fair and square boys, if you can't afford the play, don't sit down at the table," Rustin said.

"You robbed us!" one of the men said pointing a finger at him. The man was tall and thin and his finger looked bony as he struck the air with his arm. The men clearly didn't have much money as witnessed by their simple clothes, aging shoes and headwear.

"I can't help you boys much. I can't give it all back, that wouldn't be fair, but if you want a little back I bet we could come to an arrangement," Rustin said with a shrug. Farben took this moment to look around for cops or witnesses.

Without any further conversation and just a guttural battle cry led by the middleman, they rushed forward to attack I.G. Farben and Rustin Fowler. Rustin tackled the short man easily but he refused to stop, leaving Farben alone with two men at the same time. Fists flew and despite their drunken swings, the three men landed a few punches. Rustin was finally able to lay down the short man and just as Farben was about to succumb to the two men who were hanging on him in a drunken rage; Rustin came to the rescue and threw the two men into the street. Their bodies slid on the dirt for a few feet until they came to a rest, out cold from the exertion and cheap booze.

Farben saw some lights coming up the connecting road.

"Split, I'll see you at the car," Farben said, dashing down an alley. Rustin ran down the opposite street and reached the car first. He climbed in the back seat and lay down low enough so that he could see out the windows but wouldn't be immediately noticed by someone passing. A few moments later, Farben opened the front door and sat down.

"You're not thinking of going out there tonight?"

"No, but we need to get out of town for a few minutes until this hubbub dies down. We're going to take the long way back to the motel." Farben wound the car through various streets, leaving Rustin in the back to hang on while he found a quiet part of town and then started to make his way back to the highway and the motel. Farben quietly pulled the car back into the parking lot. The two men flopped down in the beds, breathing heavily. Farben was the first to assess the damage as well as clean himself up at the cold water sink. Rustin followed him and soon they were recovered enough to talk about their next plans.

"Do you think he'll strike again?"

"He might go after a bank, he might get in another fight and kill someone, he might kill someone at a bank."

"That's possible. He does have quite a reputation. Wouldn't it be a great stroke of luck if he struck again and we could be on the scene?"

"Yes, yes it would." Farben sat on the edge of the bed and pulled his pants off. His white undershirt and boxers hung on him. He looked at the floor and rubbed his hands. Rustin pulled off the last of his clothes.

"Do you want to cuddle?" Rustin offered.

Farben took a deep breath.

"Do you think we should?"

"We always do when we're on assignment like this. You know

Anna doesn't mind."

"OK."

Farben crawled into bed with Rustin and Rustin accepted him into his arms and held him tightly and tucked together the men fell into a deep sleep. Images flashed past Farben's eyes but he was not disturbed. He felt safe in Rustin's arms and was able to sleep soundly. His exemplary sleep was shattered by a frantic knock on the door. Farben was the first to hear it. His eyes popped open and he removed himself from the safe embrace. He covered Rustin back over and rolled the covers back on his bed some more and put the pillow on the floor. The person was insistent.

"Coming! Damn it." Farben moved around the end of the beds and to the door. It was the front deskman. Farben opened the door with a yawn.

"Yes, what is it?"

"He's struck again! I just heard! The Prairie Bank and Trust in St. Joseph. It's their only bank in town. He's stuck the place up, with a girl this time. She even had a gun! Have you ever heard of such a thing!"

Farben's mind was racing.

"Thank you for that. We'll get right on it. You may have cracked this case."

The hotelier smiled. Farben feigned amusement and closed the door and leaned against it. Rustin hadn't even moved. But it was important to catch the robber at the hideout. If their timing was just right they might be able to use this strike and the bartender's clue to find the man and get him back to Chicago.

Farben started shaking Rustin. "Wake up Rustin, wake up, we have to get to St. Joseph, right now."

Rustin groggily turned over and looked at Farben.

"Uh, huh, yeah..." Rustin sloppily pulled himself from the

bed. He scratched himself and went over to the cold water sink and started splashing his face and drinking from his hand.

"Do we get to eat first?"

"St. Joseph isn't far," Farben said, looking at the atlas.

Rustin pulled on his clothes and gathered his few belongings. He pulled out his razor to shave but Farben stopped him.

"Later, later, we have to go!" Rustin and Farben, barely dressed and unshaven clomped down the stairs. Farben looked at the clock, It was ten minutes after eight. Farben realized that they had slept in ninety minutes beyond their usual waking time. They soon arrived at the Packard and piled into its front seat. Rustin pulled the car back out into the street and Farben directed him east towards St. Joseph. Rustin tested the car's limit on speed. His foot was firmly planted and he passed slow traffic anywhere he could. Farben rubbed his eyes, yawned and waited for St. Joseph to come into view. He looked down at his German-made watch. Eight forty five passed as the car finally pulled into St. Joseph. It wasn't hard to find where the robbery had taken place. The town was gathered at the bank on the main street. Two local cops were standing outside trying to calm the crowd. Farben and Rustin walked up. Rustin adjusted his hat and Farben crossed his arms, trying to hear what the local police were saying.

"Please keep calm! Please keep calm! The bank will re-open later today. I'm sure Mr. Baker will be able to answer your questions about your deposits."

The crowd shouted over the cop. They were right to be concerned. A significant robbery could have ruined everyone in the town, especially if the bank had to close due to the robbery. Phrases like, "Let us in!" and "Get out of the way!" permeated the air. Farben started to muscle his way forward and Rustin followed him.

"Sir, get back in the crowd, this bank is closed."

"My name is Isaac Farben, I'm a private detective from Chicago and I'm investigating the string of robberies in the area. I'm sure your Mr. Baker will want to talk to me," he said in a smooth tone.

"That man's an investigator!" one man shouted. "He'll get to the bottom of this!" For some reason, this seemed to calm the crowd down. The cops, seeing the tide turn in their favor, ushered Rustin and Farben into the bank. The simple lobby was deserted but a quick survey told Farben everything he needed: the bullet holes in the painted plaster had caused a massive crack and the open teller cages denoted a staff on the run from danger. Like any ordinary bank, the cages were brass, the floor was an amalgam of stone and a small counter with paperwork dominated the center of the room. Some plants stood around on the edges of the modest space. Behind the teller cages, Farben could see the vault stood open - not damaged, just open. This robber was good, he had actually gotten them to open the vault. Farben couldn't help but notice the security guard shot dead on the floor, his large body crumpled in the corner.

A thin man with wire glasses appeared in a neat suit and walked towards them with his hands clasped.

"No, no, Gentlemen, the bank is closed, we've just had an incident," the man said in a high-pitched voice.

"That's what we're here about," Rustin said.

"In what capacity?" His voice was edged with indignation.

"My name is Isaac Farben, I'm a private investigator from Chicago. I'm tracking the string of robberies and I wanted to get some details, Mr. Baker is it? Your depositors outside think I'm in here to help so I think it's best that you work with me."

"Oh," he said deflated. "It was him! The man from the radio! And one of the girls went with him!" he said, lighting back up.

"I see, how much did he take?"

"$2,000," Mr. Baker replied.

"Can you cover that kind of loss?"

"It's inconvenient right now," Mr. Baker said. "I would have to call in loans or borrow from another bank if any would even consider us at this point. Oh it's very bad. I just had to close the bank. Everyone will want their money out right now, of course."

Farben looked at Rustin. Rustin pulled at his lip with his teeth and put his hands on his hips.

"Let me consult with my associate for a moment."

Farben and Rustin walked towards the door.

"How much do we care about this?" Farben said when they were alone in a hushed voice.

"It sucks for the people outside, but we get paid when we deliver this guy to KYW in Chicago. Even if we get the money, it will be days before we can get it back down here and we'd have to steal it from him before it was taken as evidence. He'll have to wait for the authorities to figure the whole situation out, if he can last that long."

"That was what I thought."

The pair returned to a nervous Mr. Baker.

"Thank you for your cooperation. We're going to see what we can do about finding him today. We have some information that will lead us to the killer."

"What should I do?" he asked as a seeming rhetorical question but seriously enough to warrant an answer from Rustin.

"Call in some loans." Rustin said over his shoulder as they departed.

Farben and Rustin reappeared on the steps of the corner bank. Farben held up his hands. He hated crowds but he knew that he needed to calm down this mob or something violent might occur.

"Everything is under control. Mr. Baker will be out shortly

and he will take care of all your needs. It was not a bad robbery. Think of your fellow man, the fellow who worked here, he's dead and that's what's important right now," Farben said.

"Take it away, boys," Rustin said as they walked back to the car.

Farben slid into the driver's seat and Rustin scooted over to the passenger side. Farben pulled out into the street and raced out of the town in a cloud. He directed the car towards where he thought the hideout was. He tracked the car northwest and took any dusty road he could. Rustin looked out the window to see if he could sight an abandoned house. Farben stopped on a small hill and looked around.

"There, over there!" Rustin said. Farben looked out and there was the peak of what looked like an abandoned house. The peak wasn't painted. Farben reached in under the driver's seat and pulled out a pair of opera glasses. The house looked abandoned enough. He looked the other way and he could faintly make out Champagne in the distance.

"I think that's it. Let's drive around." Farben pulled the car back to the last intersection going north. Rustin hung out of the car looking for any signs of the house or their quarry.

"Left!" Rustin shouted. He braced himself for a sudden turn to the left down a bad road. The car bounced and jerked around as Farben struggled to keep a straight course. Finally, after passing up and down a few shallow hills, Rustin spotted the house again. Farben had it in sight at this point and jerked the car right towards the house. No sooner had Farben stopped at the house than he spied a Dodge car sitting behind it. Farben and Rustin opened the doors and stepped out of the dusty car and looked around for signs of life. Their first sign of life was loud and cut the air like a knife. The minute the shotgun blast reached his ears Farben hit the ground like flour from a truck. Rustin laid down more carefully on the Illinois dust.

"What do you boys want!" a disembodied voice said.

Farben started to crawl up but he shot in their general direction again.

"You can tell me from down there."

"We're here, from KYW Chicago, the radio station. They heard your broadcasts from the jail you were in and they wanted to have you up to Chicago for an interview and for you to tell stories."

"On the radio!" Rustin added.

"Yes, on the radio," Farben said.

"Yall can stand up now." The voice was close, just over their heads in fact. Farben looked up at the shoes of their man. He leaned back slowly and stood up in a smooth motion. Rustin followed his lead. Before them, stood their man, Freddie Weeks.

Their man extended his hand towards Farben.

"Name's Freddie, Freddie Weeks. You got a name?"

"Isaac, Isaac Farben. Rhis is my associate, Rustin Fowler." Rustin held out his hand. Freddie shook both of their hands.

"Honey, is everything alright? Did you kill them?" came a female voice from inside the house.

"Yeah, everything's fine, babydoll, I didn't kill nobody. It's just some men from the radio station in Chicago."

A woman came out in a tunic, bed sheet and little else. Her blonde hair was close cut and curly but right now hung in a pile around her head.

"Get back in the house, honey. I'm talking to these men."

"OK," she said, pouting.

"KYW in Chicago? Wants to talk to me?"

"That's right, they heard your broadcasts from the last time you were in lockup and they wanted to get the first scoop on your latest, uh, escapade. They were also hoping for some of your stories," Farben said dusting off his tailored suit.

"Like, going to Alaska and fighting a bear and all that?"

"That's right," Rustin said.

"I'd like that a lot but I can't," Freddie started in towards the house. "Gin?"

"Yes," Rustin said, smiling.

"Come on up." Rustin and Farben walked up the weather worn steps and onto the grey porch. Freddie flung the door open and beckoned the men in.

"It's a little warm, the ice ran out yesterday," Freddie said as he handed them a jar of gin. Rustin unscrewed the top and took a nice sip.

Freddie smiled at him. "He gets the idea."

Farben looked down at the jar lifted the liquid to his lips. The harsh flavor and taste struck his tongue like a tympani at the end of a symphony. He swallowed the juniper liquid quickly.

"Welcome to our humble home, for the time being. I just found it out here. Looks like the family left in a hurry or somebody died." Freddie said swaggering around the open spaces of the house and towards the back porch.. Indeed, the house looked like it had been recently lived in. The sedate Victorian furniture and lack of dust demonstrated that someone had been there. Candle holders still held candles and many of the kerosene lamps were full of fuel. The stairs creaked as the lady of the house descended once again, in a neat tunic and drop-waist skirt with her handbag in hand. Farben and Rustin turned around just in time to see her turning the corner and coming towards them. Freddie stood in the doorway to the backyard and turned around when he heard her delicate footsteps.

"There's my girl!" Freddie said. She curled up into his arms and smiled.

"Are you guys ready to go?" Farben asked.

"Going where?" she asked, pouting again.

"They want us to come with them to Chicago so I can tell

stories on the radio."

"Oh neat!"

"We were hoping to leave sooner rather than later," Rustin added.

"Oh, but I can't possibly go to Chicago looking like this!" she replied.

"And you won't, we'll go to Chicago, Edie, buy you some new duds, get all dressed up and hit the town, then the radio. I told you I'd show you the world, didn't I?"

"You did, Daddy, you did."

"Yes!" Farben feigned agreement with the plan. "We're from there, we'll go shopping at Marshall Fields for the latest fashions."

"I think you still have to look fashionable even for radio," Rustin injected.

"As long as they are coming!" Farben thought.

"Alright, well, let me find my shirt then."

Freddie wandered upstairs and came back down with a button down shirt under his suspenders. He pulled on his shoes and grabbed a large bag out of the under-stair closet. He started towards the front yard.

"That your car out there?"

"Yes."

"She's real fine!" Freddie said swaggering down the steps towards the car. "What do I do with my car?"

"Leave it here, you can come back to get it once you've done the radio show. They might even send someone to pick it up."

Farben and Rustin, dame in tow, started towards the car. Rustin ran ahead to open the rear door of the car and pull the extra seat out of the floor. Freddie, and the lady all stepped into the car and immediately took up the back bench seat. Farben looked at the happy couple, put the extra seat back in the floor and slid into the passenger side of the front bench seat with Rustin. Rustin fired up the Packard and they set off for Chicago.

"Hey now, can we make a few stops?" Farben turned around to look towards the back seat. He motioned for Rustin to pull over.

"What stops?" Farben said once the car was on the side of the road.

"To pick up the rest of the money."

"Money? What's that in the bag?"

"That's just part of it. Here, go back a couple miles and take that dirt road, there's some I have under a tree there near this farmer's house. And then I want to pick up the gold."

"Just two stops?"

"Yeah, just these two. I don't want get too far from my money." He grabbed the girl's knee and she laughed. Farben turned around and looked at Rustin.

Rustin turned the car around and made the left turn and started rumbling down the road. The car swerved and jolted as he tried to avoid as many potholes as possible. The car kept rolling and rumbling and the happy couple in the rear kept necking.

Farben put up the screen.

"Disgusting."

"What?" Rustin shouted.

"Nothing," Farben said under his breath. He looked out to the flat prairie and fields,unbuttoned his collar and pulled down his tie. There was no need for formality out here in the freshly planted fields of southern Illinois. Only one thing mattered and that was getting this guy back to Chicago and collecting the payment from the radio station. If there were a few detours, then so be it. Farben's head swiveled around looking for what he thought might be hiding places. A large cottonwood tree that had grown near a small stream was slowly coming into view. No sooner than Farben had the tree in view then a knock on the screen came from the back. Farben lowered the screen with the little handle.

"That tree there! Stop there! Do you got anything to dig with?" Freddie said with a brown-toothed grin.

Farben tapped Rustin on the shoulder and pointed him towards the tree. Rustin pulled the car up to the tree and it rolled to a stop. The dust cloud behind them fell around the car and the party disembarked from the car.

"You got anything to dig with?" Freddie repeated, as he looked up at the tree and started walking towards the tree across the green grass that surrounded it.

"No, not really," Farben said.

"Maybe the tyre iron," Rustin said. "We can use it as a pick and move the loosened dirt with our hands."

"Sounds good, gentlemen! Let's get to work!" Freddie said, removing his shirt. Rustin dug around the trunk of the car and retrieved the tyre iron and joined Freddie under the tree. Freddie started in with the tyre iron while Rustin removed the dirt with his hands and after a few minutes, Freddie put down the tyre iron and they dug down to the burlap sack that held the money. He lifted it out of the hole and held it up for Edie to see. She clapped and jumped up and down from the lowered rear window of the car.

Farben leaned against the hood with his arms crossed and looked at Rustin and Freddie lowering the money into the trunk of the car.

"Where to next?" Farben said. "You said there were a few stops." No sooner were the words out of Rustin's mouth than a shotgun blast pierced the air. Farben and Rustin jolted towards the big tree to see an aging farmer in dirt stained overalls holding a gun and stumbling towards them. Farben held up his hands with Rustin following the motion. Freddie held his hands out for a moment.

"Hey, Hey, don't shoot man, don't shoot!" Freddie said.

"You tryin' to take my money!"

"It's not your money, sir, it belongs to me. My name is Freddie."

"Say, you the Freddie in the paper?"

"Yessir, that's me."

"Then I'll be doing the county a favor by filling your ass with lead!"

"No sir! I have a lady in the car. You don't want to shoot!"

The farmer was not convinced and moved closer. Freddie opened the bag and took out a pile of bills.

"How about some money? Why don't you take some? This will set you up real good," Freddie said, extending his arm with the cash in hand. He threw it on the ground towards the farmer. The farmer picked up the money and looked at it and stuffed it in his overalls.

"See, all you had to do was ask," Freddie said.

The farmer dropped his weapon.

"Y'all be gettin' up outta here now."

"Sure, sure, we're going," Freddie said, slowly backing away towards the car.

He looked around as he buttoned his cotton shirt and stuffed it in his pants.

"Nah, this works. I'll come back for the gold bars later. I don't need to carry all my money at once. Let's get up to Chicago. Edie needs to shop for some new clothes and I'll be mighty hungry."

Farben shrugged his shoulders and opened the door to get back into the car. Freddie jumped back in and seated himself next to the dame.

"Oh, you smell so manly!" she exclaimed crossing her ankles.

"We'll get up to Chicago and get a bath, new clothes, and hit the town for some dancin',"

Farben put the screen up again and looked at Rustin. Rustin started the car, turned it around and started bouncing down the road again.

Rustin guided the car back to the highway and once they arrived at Highway 45 Rustin put all twelve cylinders to work to get to Chicago before anyone changed their minds. By late afternoon, the group pulled into Chicago. Rustin guided the Packard towards the shopping district where the fashionable stores were. Rustin parked the car in front of Marshall Fields and quickly got out and pulled open the door for Freddie and company. Farben followed and leaned towards him.

"Stay with the car," Farben intoned as he led them through the rotating doors into the department store.

The doorman greeted Farben as he stepped into the gleaming interior

"Here we are."

"Oh! Look at all these pretty things! And perfume! I need a new fragrance!" Edie exclaimed, clasping her hands to her chest.

"You can get anything you like, baby!"

"Yes, uh, um, what did you say your name was?" Farben said leaning towards her.

"Edie, Edie Rainier."

"Miss Rainier." Farben said her name with a musical tone in his voice. No sooner than the introduction was made she was off in a flash, plucking at fabric and keeping the attendants running around the store finding things. Soon, she was holed up in a dressing room fitting herself into gowns, dresses, and hats. She stood in front of the five way mirror examining each item like a seasoned shopper and picking out only the best, and from what Farben could tell from the price tags, the most expensive items. Farben left her with the attendants and Freddie to see

Rustin for a moment.

Rustin was sitting in the car looking up and down the street.

"What are you looking for?" Farben asked, leaning into the passenger window.

"Cops."

"They don't even know we're here, as far as they know, we're just here shopping."

"Right."

"Anyway, they are going to want to go out afterwards. I need you to go home, get us tuxedos and bring them back here. Also, call and reserve my table at Cafe Sheridan and find a show or something to go to. I'm going to phone KYW and let them know we have him and that we can bring him in tonight at 8 p.m."

"Anything else?"

"No. Get moving, we've got to move fast for this to work!"

Farben slapped the side of the car. Rustin nodded his head and fired up the engine and pulled out into traffic. Farben revisited the happy couple inside. Freddie piled more items on the counter and the clerks were busily tallying up the total. Farben smiled at them and found a phone booth in the lobby.

"Hello? Yes Operator? Yes, get me KYW in the Com Ed building, yes, thank you." Farben waited a moment for the call to be connected.

"KYW, Chicago."

"Hello? This is Isaac Farben speaking, please put me through to Mr. Searlye. It is urgent that he speak with me."

"Who did you say was calling?" the other end of the phone said.

"Isaac Farben!"

The line was silent for a moment.

"Searlye here."

"Hello, Mr. Searlye, It's Isaac Farben here. I have him, I'll have him for the evening broadcast. He has a girl with him, we're going to get some dinner and then we'll be by."

"Good, I'll put the cops on standby."

"Do you want a real story?"

"Always."

"I'll tell you where to have him arrested. We'll be at the Cafe Sheridan for dinner and then we'll be at a show after the radio interview. If you want a big story, have him arrested there, it'll make the papers and your station will be all over the news."

The line was silent for a moment. "Let's do it."

"Alright, I'll see you in a few hours."

Farben took this private moment to sample some of the liquid in his ankle flask. It had been a long day and he was getting dangerously close to sober. Farben wiped his mouth and walked back upstairs to the couple. The clerk had just finished making out the ticket. The clerk was a mousy looking woman with glasses and curled hair in a modern style. She had just finished presenting the bill to Freddie. He started to dig in the bag.

"That won't be necessary."

"What do you mean? I gotta pay this bill."

Farben looked at the clerk. "My name is Isaac Farben, I have an account here, you can put it on that."

"Oh, Mr. Farben, very good then, your personal account or your father's?"

"My own, thank you." Farben bristled at the mention of his father or his Marshall Fields account.

Freddie leaned against the counter as Edie kept looking at her new fur.

"Well, well, Mr. Farben, you ain't just no gum shoe are you? You're a big deal."

Farben smirked a bit. "I suppose."

"Put it on my account, please," Freddie smirked at his own sarcasm. "Come on, they don't do that for just anybody. And who is your father?"

"That's not important, he's just a businessman. Let's get these things wrapped up and get ready for the evening. We're due at the ComEd Building around 7, just in time to get ready and eat at the Cafe Sheridan." Farben and the party, packages in hand, piled into the Packard and raced for Farben's apartment to prepare the evening, eat at the Café Sheridan and make the drive to ComEd.

"And that's how I killed a bear in Alaska." Freddie leaned into the microphone.

"That's fantastic, really fantastic. What has you going on your current crime spree?"

"I wouldn't call it a crime spree. I separated a bank from its money."

"Yes, but what about the depositors? What about their money?"

Freddie shrugged. "I don't know, I don't really care. I just want to have a good time, get a good woman around me. Like this one right here." Freddie hugged Edie close. Farben and Rustin stood outside the booth and looked at the couple huddled up to the microphone as the announcer interviewed them.

"What a ham," Rustin remarked.

"Yeah," Farben replied, arms crossed. His wrist crinkled the paper of the cheque in his breast pocket; $1,500 for delivering a man to a radio station to tell stories and get arrested.

"What are you going to do about that bill at Marshall Fields?" Rustin replied.

"It's on my account, I'll obviously pay it." Farben said. "Besides, Anna will need to get us that radio soon and we may as well pay it on time."

"She'll love that."

"Look smart, they're coming out."

Rustin and Isaac whisked the party off to the club for drink and dancing and the pay off.

Back at Isaac's apartment, Anna gathered up the last towels and took them towards the laundry basket to send out for launder. She had just enough time to get herself ready to meet Rustin and Isaac at the theatre. She slipped out of her dress and adjusted her brassiere and stockings as she plucked out a sequined dress. She held it up first and admired it and then stepped into it. The tunic and skirt from the day time flopped on the bed. Modest heels and a tasseled hat completed her evening look and she descended the elevator to the street to look for a taxi. She held out her hand and a small yellow taxi soon pulled over. Anna flung open the door and slid into the seat. The taxi deposited her at the Manhattan club. She paid and tipped the cabbie and closed her purse and made her way into the club. As she opened the decorative handle on the door she saw four uniformed Chicago policeman walking up the sidewalk. She smiled and scooted across the thick carpet to buy a ticket for the show. She took her ticket and walked in looking for her men and the couple who soon would be relieved of their seats by the Chicago police. Then she stood aside as the police hustled Freddie and his accomplice out of the theatre. The players recaptured the crowd and the show continued into the night.

"Just one more loose end," Farben thought, as his head hit the pillow that night.

The drive didn't seem as long this time, as they made their way down to the small farming community of St. Joseph. When I.G. and Rustin arrived, the manager of the St. Joseph Bank and Trust was sitting in his office looking at his balance sheets when he heard a knock on the door. He stood up, adjusted his coat and walked towards the door waving his hands. "We're closed today!"

Rustin was insistent and kept knocking. The bank manager peered through the door and recognized him. He unlocked the door and opened it a bit.

"Yes?"

"Hello, you may remember me. I was here with another man the other day. We were looking for Freddie Weeks?" Rustin said.

"Yes, yes, come in quickly."

Rustin walked into the bank and put the heavy burlap sack on the floor.

"I think you'll find everything in order."

"What do you mean?"

"This is your money, isn't it?"

"Uh, are you sure that's all our money? What about the other banks he robbed?"

Rustin shrugged his shoulders. "He probably spent most of that. This was mostly the only money he had. I would say that you've lucked out."

The bank manager opened the sack to look at the wrapped bills. He picked up the sack and smiled.

"I'll put an announcement in the paper. Who should I say did this for our town?"

"Freddie Weeks."

Rustin walked out of the bank and out into the dusty street. Hands in pockets, he looked around at the townspeople going about their business until he heard a tapping on glass.

Farben leaned out of the window in the back of the Packard.

"Alright, we've done our good deed, now get me back to Chicago, small towns are weird. People are…Nice."

Rustin smiled and removed his hands from his pockets and walked over to the car, climbed in the front seat and put the wheels moving to Chicago. Farben let the gentle rocking back and forth of the car lull him into a day-time doze.